I0787942

PARK BENCH STORY's By Announimis

Manojlo Desovski

PARK BENCH STORY's
By Announimis

MD

Common Room/ 52-62 John Street,

Erskineville NSW 2043

Ph: 02 9557 58 34

Mob: 0011 61 403 965 118

Email: infomd82@gmail.com

Information

Language: English

Category: Comedy/Romance/Fiction/Drama

Author: Manojlo Desovski

Editor: Manojlo Desovski

Graphic Design: Manojlo Desovski

Self Published: 01/11/15

ISBN-13:978-0-9953982-0-7

CIP:

NLApp64521

CHAPTER 1 PARK BENCH STORY's

MATE OF OURS

"My mate and I, were driving on yet another 'Win', another mutual getogether of soul mates.

Anyways, "not my story to tell, but I'm telling anyways, as was there as well"

Driving with mate towards the house of mate's girlfriend to drop him off, for the usual yet again, bumping and grinding.

Was the moment of, " listen hear, stay hear with the car, I'le be back in 45 to an hour.

I'm like, "sure don't have much else to do, may as well".

'20min' later, climbing out 'only the ground floor window', but run's out this 'Huge' mate with nothing on but his birthday suit. LOL

Running 'full blast', holding his junk along the way.. Then 'bouncing' as he gets to the grass, careful he doesn't step on any 'bindis'.

Jump's in the car, Drive!!!, Drive!!!, Drive!!! Go Go!, Go!
'I'm driving, I'm driving'.

'What happened' ?

He says the mother heard them bumping and grinding, went to the kitchen got the knife and chased him out."

The End

FIRST PLACE CERTIFICATE

"We were given a task to raise funds for the school; the product we were selling was chocolates. Sure enough, I saw an opportunity for 'making money' and 'eating chocolate', 'woo wee'. Win Win, we have a saying, "as playing the violins and getting paid for it" lOL, only in Australia loL.

Anyways, I was given a full box and tolled "sell as many as you can and bring back the rest".

On my way back from school, I started door knocking, my first ever experience, (actually not really, had experience from trick or treating few years back, but first experience apart from trick or treating. Or is knock and run, but first legit business door knocking.

Knock! knock!, knock! knock!, urges to do the runner loL, answer at the door..

The Spil; My name is, I am from, we are doing a fund raiser would you like to donate and help our cause ?

[With the cutest puppy face ever and I did it with the whole area.. Had a good strike rate thinking back.. Apart from the no one home houses and hardly anyone turned me back.]

On and on it went for days, as it was pretty scary after sun had gone down, wasn't taking that risk on my own, so had to call it quits after sundown.

Only bad thing is 'every' time I'd sell a 'bar', I'd treat myself a 'bar' talk about getting high on your own supply.

Sold six big boxes and have the best memory of the chocolate fix ever, all the money was accounted for even the one's me and the 'Fam' kept eating, made a killing.

Woo wee, 'First Prize' for fund raising."

The End

FIRST PRIZE FOR COMEDY IN DRAMA

"We all had to mime a story.

Hard to tell as it was all miming, but it was a simple story of sitting on the floor, picking a four leaf clover and getting good luck."

The End

SWIMMING

"Month's and months, year's and year's after school work came, 'Swimming Training'.

It's a great relaxing and very healthy sport, some say, 'boring' and for 'girls', but there's all sorts of styles: water polo, diving, uni sync dancing, and 'Free Style'; 100m, 2 laps, 200m, 4 laps, 400m, 8 laps and 1500m, 30 laps.

[With the closest feeling of actually flying, and the dreams you get of flying as a kick backs, I was warming up for the Olympics.]

Man the coach use to work us hard, everyone gather around, today;

1) 100m warm up Freestyle,
2) 400m sprint Freestyle
3) 200m warm up Backstroke
3) 1500m Freestyle, I'm timing you
4) 200m Butterfly
5) 1000m Mix

All in under an hour. That's what Olympians train on, you'd get to the break, want to catch your breath, as you're out of breath to say you're out of breath. "What you doing here ? off you go, come on come on, your lagging" .. I'm coming 2nd I'm lagging he goes, felt like jumping out and putting him in the water .. however kept swimming of-course.

[For good reasons he use to say that, I later with time learnt, good coach man thinking back.] However still had a gut like me now, like most men in their, 'Dirty 30's'.

The final day I had the shits, I walked off saying, you want 10,000m you jump in and do them,

"I'd like to know why your gut's so big and how you feel it's ok to preach this talk.. A good coach would come in and swim these laps with us, I quite this Jaz". He was ready and taking off his shirt, I did the runner .'

Man I felt terrible for years in late adulthood when I put on a bit of weight."

The End

TIME TO THINK

Soon enough, I had time to 'think' and 'focus' on "relaxing and hanging out with mates and dating chicks cuz".

The End

AFTER THE FACT

"Soon after that; nights where becoming slow and boring. 'Was thinking I'm faster than the rotation of the earth, LoL '

I got 'lucky' and got a mad job after school hours at a 'Video Arcade'.

All the games you could dream of, 'dream of': Daytona, Sega Rally, Street Fighter, NBA Jam, Soccer, Athletics, Point Blank, you name it 'we', mate's and Co' had it."

The End

VIDEO ARCADE CENTRE

"On and on it went, tick tock', tick tock' as the clock strikes, so did the days of our lives.

(It became one of the main, local [hang out's] 'not too wise a business man, those days, but smarter than me now... ')

Hang out's along with [PCYC] my chosen and registered as member club and the [J's Centre], [The Parks], [Land's] [Ocean's] and [Lookouts].

Video Arcade: 'Replay', as the hang out, touched on all areas of Civil Fun and Criminal Fun, that's the pie isn't it, 100% the people with money to play these expensive $2.00, 5 min games.

From; 'Pick pocketing' to 'weapons', to 'drugs', to 'grand theft auto's' to 'stand over's' to 'extortion's', to 'plain thieving', to 'other', there was a weekend for everything.

Along that was 'celebration drink up's, get together and party's'.

"Everyone was lucky go merry.."

The End

MRX

GRAND THEFT

This one's from the 'books', one that's approved. It was a cool summer night, "not a reaches story or one I condone but a funny one".

By now the hip thing in was to 'drive', have your own car or not, the thing was 'cruising and driving around'.

Well as, X________ mate 1, had no license and no car; he thought it would be a good idea to pinch one, [get a hotty], and go driving that night!! of-course to return it in the morning.

Cool, calm and collected, hair done, swave; Good bloke by all means, but temptation in that case, stops by the shop, in a white X________ Beep, Beep, Beep, car running and standing position.

I'm like who's this beeping outside like a lunatic ...

Hurry, Hurry, come see my new hotty, (proud as anything)

"Who wants to go cruising tonight" ??

(On duty at the time), "would love to, but working right now, pick me up after work yea, I finish 12am".

Ps "could you please move your car little down the road so it's not in front of the business? [Sure enough he does, while waiting for 5 volunteers, to jump in]."

Wooooot woooooot, "pull over", the local police car Syrians.

FUCK, my mates a goner, I thought, 'that's it, charged and jail, I thought, I froze myself on his behalf, choked and couldn't think of a way out, Red Handed, his done.

Walk's out the copper; not knowing what's going on, "hands on the steering wheel" so he does...

The second he gets close enough to car, to be furthest away from his car, without seeing his face... Foot on the pedal; 'Gun's' it 5 seconds Quarter mile, left fishes and skid marks... away from the police.

Now, the policeman's running back to his car, jumps in his driver seat; wooooot woooot, sirens and reporting in pursuit of a young male, white X________ model. Full fledged car chase in the middle of Town.

The next day the story goes, they drove around for 15 min, chasing each other through street's and laneways and roundabouts and through building complex driveways and front and back entry's, sheer local knowledge of the streets, out maneuvers them through a Cul-de-sac st, leading to a park, waking up the hole neighborhood by his beeping, jumping out running through the park, leading to his front door, running upstairs, changing to PJ's and coming back out, portending to be woken up, along with half the neighborhood, what happened hear officers ??

They never caught the driver, till now maybe."

The End
MRX

PISSING IN THE WIND

"It was a holiday in the mad town of Gosford. 'Drunk as Tits' as the saying goes.. is that a saying? Drunk as Tit's ? yes it is.

[Time to go bathroom], House too far away, as where hanging on the hill of a park, watching the beauty of, 'Gosford Star Filled Sky'.

Flop it out, and go... 'Wooooshka the wind', "piss blocked and suspended in mid air to spray back, all back over me" and my other mate had the same experience as one other was laughing at us."

The End

SPITTING IN THE WIND

"The funniest of events, 'was' a bit of a spitter in my youthful days, but who wasn't, even Leo from Titanic, was; and was hardly ever disgusting or on 'purpose' ok empty one's where.

"We were driving 80 k's at least, It was a highway, I was in the passenger seat, open the window, flooop spit out the window, 'wak' like bullet back in my direction spray in the face. Lol."

"Talk about spitting in the wind".

The End

CANBERRA Y 9 NHSPA SCIENCE EXCURSION

Gagged/ Engaged/ Approved

Sitting at the park bench again

"Oooh it was a wild and beauty of a day and night.

'Bus Drive' was average but excitement levels where 'off the chart'.

Think I forged my permission slip that trip, close to missing out I was loL, but the old 'mastering' Dad's signature and 'Power of Attorney' as well, prevailed..

Anyways, I'm sure and think there were one or two other people in the same boat.., Lol, as remember them going to the girls bathroom 'even' to forge it, LOL. "You can never be too low key"

So we stopped at the 'BaaaBaaa Sheep Shop' in Canberra and had our quick lunch break.

The Telescope, 'woooweee', it was 'huge', I zoomed in with my supervision, (the observatory was white and oval in shape)   [Loved Science], 'put that one in the long term memory' (It was a clear black night).
Long story short, everyone had a turn at looking through the eye peace, zooming in and focusing and remember for the first time, seeing a full planet/(world) (close up), Mars'.

"I was excited, that's for sure, It won't be long before we see Alien's or Other planets on earth or somewhere" [I gave it 15 to 20 years loll].

Anyway's the day passed and it was a stay over excursion. Beauty of Cabins, nice timber and weather board finish, 'from memory' cute and in fantastic organized positioning.

We all rushed inside, each to their own cabin, and only know bits and pieces from others; but ours was: B_____, R______, C_______, K__, Me, and I________Mate 6.

Each grabbing a bunk bed, cheering and excited. Remember grabbing a bottom bunk, (Top bunk more popular but experience knows bottom bunk better), and lucky I did as later story will reveal.

Unpacked and bags under beds, 'warnings' flying for no stealing amongst friends.

Little tired, we all relaxed, 'I did anyways in my own little world', for a while..

Night came, full of sugar and energy, no teachers in sight, 'after my careful sussing out'. However/but knowing there hiding and in stand by somewhere.

First or after can't remember; however came the 'pillow fight'.. 'Man' got wacked over the head by B____, 'Wack' again, 'Boom', I go "if it's pillow fights I'm in" I'le show you, get my pillow jam it tight, 'half inside good sleve grip' (from experience) and 'wak' we started. Boom, 'wack' from R_____, in the head and face, 'Wack' to B______ as pay back, 'Wack' C______ Jumps in.. Wak K____ jumps in , Man he was good... Wak Wak Wak Wak; on we went till we where rect..

Cooling off and calling time out, we all settled down and chilled..

Moments later, K____ and I got the boredoms, 'Mischief' little things, we where.. What to do.. Look out the window, wow-owe, "Girls Cabin" right across ours... [Full, 6 Chicks Cabin, without parents or teachers, me and K______ went bonkers.]

Calling R_____ and B_______to share and support. We wave hi, whistling and waving. Girls respond in full kindness, waving and saying hi back, 'remember J_____ Miss 1, A______Miss 2, M______ Miss 3, T______ Miss 4, ?______Miss 5, ?_______ Miss 6 hard to tell as they where 100M away and looking through a square window and they were all squished'.

What to do we do, the old 'Mate X', "show us you're Tits"..

Lights 'flashing' on and off, on and off, on they went' (curtains drawn full back), 'Boooom,

Interruption by Hotty Chick as writing and telling this story, just like the real life stories.

(Shhhhhhh)

Yes, 'Boom', the girls 'flashed' us all, bam we were cheering, they took shirts of and everything.

'We sort of choked in the moment thinking back now' but R_______ took his shirt off, me in singlet, K____ in shirt.

From there, C______ , K_______, and I wanted to journey some more. We did the open door, tip toe forward, sprit blast as soon as the teachers back is to us...

Vooom Ken first, Vooom Me, Vooom Cam,

Actually Cam let me go ahead before him and then sprinted way past me, all to the fact of running so fast, like lightning, this wasn't funny, but funny now, 'Wam' 'Somersault', body going forward, legs going up in the air, I'm thinking a Ghost got him, there was nothing there, no wall, no fence, no nothing just black night, space and the cabin, only for me to slow down right at him and realize a 'Rope' across the path..

Cam steady and calm, "I'm all right" he says, I'm in shock, but comforting and looking out "we hear and see" A, Teacher's flash light, 'FLASH', all three of us 'bolting' back to our Cabin as 'Rules' no going out of Cabin; knowing detention's and suspension's will fly. Bolting back... doors open and waiting, woom 'lasta' jump, (fly chest first in my bunk), shoes on and all, under blanket, covered head to toe, portending to sleep.

In comes the 'Torch', 'Flash' "have you been outside" (no reply by me, holding my breath, so don't breath heavy, cooling off... 'Hmmm I'm sleeping..' "Oh, ok, sorry, go back to bed".

Didn't move from bed all night..

They had to use 'Rope's and Barb Wires' to manage us Teenagers."

The End

"Funny story, (on break from working at the park bench, one from long time ago).

Life lesson, Mischiefi.

'Once upon a time, many, many, years ago while in school was in an Anonymous class and was given an assignment to do, loL'. The assignment was simple a page story or two on an 'article'. Long story short, I was short for time that day, 'rarely' however happens.

I relied, shouldn't rely, but did on a good friend to help out. Was so short on time and silly mistake too, but copied the assignment 'Word for Word', and handed in.

The day our assignments where marked, 'poor buddy got the LECTURE/DETENTION, why did you copy M's work ? ' LoL, but I stepped in and explained'."

The End

"(Along side, at 'par' with four or five other nights, and the story's I'm telling', this would have been one of my deepest, deepest, laughs in life.

I'm pretty sure it was a Saturday night or could have been Friday or Sunday; but the weekend I'm pretty sure.

Hun, decided to introduce me to a Comedy Festival.

I was 'impressed', 'thinking back now it was pretty 'pricy' entry fee, but anyways we could afford it at the time').

'Fox Studios, man did I say 'Live Stand Up' at Fox'.

'The night was going along smoothly, we got nice seats and listening to The Professional. I say a Professional as always been B+ Student, remember the plots but never the titles, okay, [Stand up Live] Performing, what am I a Computer, 'Moe' it was too, LOL, who could tell park bench story's and jokes for real LOL.

He touched on all areas, but he focused on: 'Marriage' and 'Relationships'.

He was telling a story on how his life is influenced and how he has it hard, because his married.

"My wife makes me report every time I go to the bathroom". I'd be in the bathroom, she'd be like "you didn't report today!!!".

"At that time he must have hit the mark, as I had an influx of memories pop up, and just pissed myself, laughing out loud"."

The End

GHETTO

"Once upon a time, VERY, VERY long time ago, 'we', 'us' found ourselves in a house in the Ghetto.

We, my mate S______ and I, me and my mate S______, were too young to hang out with the big boys; but we were old enough and smart enough to listen in from the next room.

What was funny was, that: one, we were a little 'high' on the weed, but more so, what I remember making me laugh was: 'hear was one of the most Notorious OG's in the County, yet his yelling and screaming top of his lungs, telling an X rated 'Gun Robbery' gone Wrong. "How he's pulled out the gun, had no bullets for warning shots and had to do the runner."

The End

DROPPING ON THE FLOOR

"During the 'Replay' day's there was something funny said by my older brother.. All I remember was falling down on the floor and rolling laughing out loud'" LoL.

THE PARK

"The night at park, 'little drunk' and 'spiked' for sure, thinking back... was park just next to Newtown/Erko Oval.

We tried, laying down on the floor, looking straight up, straight at the night sky, for the first time's.

All of sudden the funniest 'accents' and the word 'Wok'.

"Just made us lough out loud".

(It was a clear night and stars where out)"

BALL FIGHT

"(There were about 20 people, G________ started it all, we where spreading and shuffling the teddy bears and yellow smiley faces with stickers which can be exchanged for free games, from the metal claw games).

'In flys in G________, shoulder charges me, pushes me out of the way; grabs a shirt full and starts pegging it at people's heads. Free games, free games; Balls bouncing of heads, and their pegging them right back at us. I see the fight starting, stack up my shirt, start pegging and going full blast, 30 min yellow ball, pegging at heads and dodging of balls fight. Flying through the air from good distance, like a skirmish ball fight.
Laughing to the max every single through. LoL.

URBAN LEGEND WHY

"This an actual 'urban legend', or was it one of us Anonyms ?.

'It started during the HSC Exams'.

The 'Final Exam' for the 'English/3 Unit Class' was to write an essay of a 1000 words on the topic, 'WHY' ?

'The bell for the, (pens down), went off'.

They collected all the papers from each student.

At the marking of papers there was one outstanding student, who got 100% and top marks.

All he wrote down on the piece of paper was "WHY NOT" and that's it.

Makes me crack up and still laugh till this day.

Reminder don't try this at home. "

THE SOLDIER

"There was a Soldier going for a Job.

On the day of the interview, the Boss say's so what can you tell me about yourself?

Well, this and that so and so.

I see..

Soldier say's one other thing you should know about me, when I was in the army, a bomb exploded near my hand, and now I've lost my thumbs.

"Ohhh", he says, "not to worry though, you got the job, however in your case you come in at 10am as all us Agents do from 9am to 10am is twiddle our thumbs."

The End

"There was, three people on the plain. The Pilot says to the people listen let's play a little game.

They say sure what we going to play.

Lets through one thing out the plain, a thing our countries have in abundance in that we have a tone of for the people on the land so they may have something.

The First person says sure ok, woweee there goes my nice silver watch. .

The Second person, woweee, there goes gold out the window.

The Third person I'm were kind of poor but you come here, grabs the first person and kicks him up the ass out the door.

Second person asks Abe why did you through him out the window.

Abe we have a lot of people in our country."

The End

3 PEOPLE ON A BRIDGE

"There were 3 People standing on a bridge, they all look down and say wow it's pretty far down there.

One says lets flop them out and see who's got the biggest

Sure enough

One flops it out says there we go not bad ay

Second one flops it out says there we go, oooh waters cold can feel the water

Third one flops it out says there we go, oooh it's sure is cold, it's deep too."

The End

LOOKING UP IN THE SKY
SMELLING THE ROSES

A, Saturday 25/04/15, DE, Issue 253, Sydney NSW

"It was a quite warm and cool night. I was finishing up from a long night walking and exercising
and bird watching.

I sat down to relax, Zzzzuuuuueeeeeemmmmm, shooting star through the sky night space.
'Nice' and 'Vivid' too, 'Bright yellow', only from corner of eye and memory of corner of eye
noticed it fading into our galaxy and after split second or two flying in the space fading away and
fizzling out.

Usually a happy moment but writing down makes me sad, a star is gone that night .

Talking about shooting Stars, "did you see or hear about the best one, I have ever seen", (LOL at
my own Grammar) although this part's correct, was the clear night hanging at The Park, looking
straight ahead and wooooshka, "twin shooting stars falling from the heavens".

"Two stars falling from the heavens"."

The End

First Time

"Talking about stars the first one I ever saw I would have been around 10 or 11 Years old. I was
always looking up in the sky hoping to hear a voice and answers from God, I do it often but at 4
out of the 5 Times its bean God can you hear me.

The other two times I know it's been two feels like two but can't remember the moments. Split
seconds of natural wonders."

The End

HAPPY DAYS

I'd get to my personal super stories of mine and you may be tired of listening to the good old growing up days however hears one from the scrap book few day's back.

It must have been summer, as the whole town was out.

From the youngest in the crew/group to the oldest in the crew/group.

It was a summer night I'm remembering, we got together for the ritual bench park not story but get together, after checking out the 10 hot spots as no mobiles to call your friends and catching up all at 5 min from each other at the 7th hang out for a drink up.

Ok it was a time with mobiles but we all met up within the same time and started at same time on the same level.

Oh my god, did we drink that night some may not remember this one however we somehow after all that ended up walking to Local Oval.

Part of City of Sydney and old Camper down Farm had the latest oval and newest running track.

This oval was like nothing I have ever seen before, it was huge, huge, among the biggest in the 100 something councils I've heard of and visited few and it was open at night.

It was late night 12pm around and stars where out bright...

A shout out of no wear let's do a 100m Sprint Run across from one end to the other.

The elite athletes and each one of us was from different areas of sport but among that night were elite professional Sprinters.. 15 of us at same time jump up and rush race to the starting line, like stampede of Bulls, Horses and Paralympians.

At the start line coached by professional, breather and loosen up and stretch.. 100m sprint, timed by stop watch, and last one is Buying a Case of Beer Bet...

At your marks, get set, Go

Man flash lighting of the start Jamie the oldest mind you takes the lead, C__________
 R1____________ can't remember who was in front of who R1________/ C__________ or C________
/R_________but they where gunning it.. Not far behind from the three where the rest of old school,
there surprised at their speed among the adrenalin of the Race... me too, blitzing through the air
and I'm not usually a fast runner although have been light on my feet on some occasions. There
was no wind to resist our traction it was an undens undanced clear night.

Most of us made it to the end if not all but remember one or two jokers I'm too drunk running's
no good or something.

Man we jumped at excitement at end of run and toasted more in the night.

We knew we'd remember that night that's for sure there was magic amongst that night."

The End

SOCCER GAME

"It was one of those days everyone was itching to be outside and hang out in the outdoors. Earge's and bonds seeking company.

A sunny weekend.

Charged up and well rested; one by one, two by two, four by dozen we arrive at the famous E_____ P_____

Private Property, No Trespassing Sign.

Jump over the fence, every one of they're own specialist professional crook technique.

Run up and two feet scrounged over fence and land

Hop up one leg up sitting on ass then follow through

Hop up, push up, leg on fence, spring jump off and land.

The ninja hectic jump wile waist on fence, right hand low on fence steady hold, force and balance, feet 180' over head land, hop bounce and steady.

Some the hand firm on fence, hop and lift two feet over fence.

Some through the entry.

Other

It was sure to turn out for a good game of Soccer, Footy, Cricket, and Olympics

"What you's training for boy's"

"Training for the Olympics "

Ref whistle without a tool, street natural.

Select your captains

Heads or tails who picks first,

Tails, "Got it" "Ok, you pick first", Na, you pick first you one fair and square "It's ok you can go" It's cool"

Ok, I pick can't remember, I remember I was one of the last in this one game though, was selected 3rd or fourth, but go na man trust me, I play for what ever's left after everyone's chosen. I knew I stunk at soccer, (as sprain injury in young days, injuring spirit) but it was happy days and joined the party rather than cheerleading with the girls like I love doing.

The game was assume, 11 on 11 full team Erko Public.

Anywhere you turn, there's a man.

Shirts V's No Shirts

Always moving trying to open up, but like glue man, just won't give in.. not even a ball with us but just kept following me worse then when I go clubbing..

After a while, I tried reasoning with him, he eased up a little.

Red shirt, gray shirt, singlet, all sorts 22 players in a 62m 1000 sqm of hilly and slumps and holes in the ground field.

B_____ as he runs through an intercept leading the pack front and centre rows behind him on each side as he jolted forward in motion, running foot work out performs and passed the opposition; strike at goal and goals it was.

"Yeeeeeeeeeeaaaaaaaaaaaaaaaaa" as we cheered'

The End

THE BASKETBALL TOURNAMENT

"It just came to me, (popped in mind), while reflecting over some other memories, however it's only that, a faint memory; of a good time. It's popped in my head many times before and cherish it dearly always wanted to write this one in particular hear goes.

It was the Number 1 centre, the headchorters.

It was after months and moths of playing basketball and training for the NBL, it was an annual thing, but the first for me, registrations for tournament .

Street Basketball 5 on 5 with 5 substitutes .

More can be said about this day however the day finally came and we were at 'Darling Harbour' on a 'hot' bright sunny day.

Half courts positioned and in row as far as the eyes could see.

Brand new, good quality, bright and colourful, sponsors and partners, The Harbour Fourshore Authorities and fresh new court lines and marks on the concrete, just for us.

X_________ PCYC v X_______ PCYC Round 1

In a controlled half court space, 5 on 5 professional basketball players, D_______, V_______, C_____ R_______ and M______

Check

One two, one two, run up and light lay up.

2 points

Check

One two one two pass; one two, pass; one two one two pass; back to centre, position him self, run up, ally op by R jump up by C and slam dunk by C_____

2 points

Check

One two, under legs, one two, criss crossing legs as ball bouncing under legs, ball control by R_____ showing of a little,

Jump up and shoot, nothing but net, 3 points off the 3 point line.

3 points

Check

Jump up and shoot, 3 point line, however 'nothing but air', (a brick).

(Opposition Ball)

Check

3 point line, shoot at basket, nothing but net, 3 points.

Check

Now was my turn to shine, defense, running putting pressure, trying get them to slip up; intercept and steal.. One two, (fuck this, too much pressure pass too centre)

Back to the centre

Centre signaling in code, 3 understand, 2 dazed, something going down.

Positions

Fake pass, two step run up and jump up slam dunk by D______

2 points

Check

5 minutes up

The winners are X_______ PCYC

That's how it was to the finals and do or dies.

At the finals for the title, shaky knees and pressure we chocked.

However we snap out of the zone turn around and see a whole, 'Darling Harbour' scenery unlike any street tournament ever recorded, (Above the Rim and all). Further locals, tourist and people had been cheering us on and clapping on what a mad performance we put on; us just calling it a day, better luck next year.

To celebrate getting that far in the tournament and with the summer heat... Gee ourselves up and jumping into the actual Harbour we went.

One by one, two after 3, off the peers and to nose dives, cooling off, in and out; in and out; until we spotted the jelly fish."

The End

DRUNKEN FOOTY

By now we were worn out and out of shape but give us a case of beer and we'll polish it in under 5 minutes.

They as I wasn't part of this competition, (focused on academic studies as story will tell) formed a local team try and revive the Newtown Jets.

Every Weekend they'd show up and play, competition level weekend touch Footy.

If they won one game id say hi and say good job

Smokers, alcoholics, pimps and players, unfit buy year.

However they got fitter and fitter, if they plaid on we would have got back to our former glory days, ended up somewhere had local business sponsorship and all, jerseys and all.

One final indoors friendly for good old times sake, between ourselves.

10 on 10 touch footy at the indoors basketball court, shirts as goals and perimeter the fields.

Coin Toss for Ball.

'Kick off' Drop kick bom high in the air.

Sprinting to the other side, ball still in air there all waiting for it to drop; good catch and touched.

Positions, tap and play.

Run up.. chip kick, sprint to catch ball however missed opportunity that time, ball out.

Positions, '20 meter restart', which was 10 in this game, 'tap and play'.

Run up, gain some ground, pass run up fake pass, side step, hustle, nowhere to go and tap.

Positions tap and play on and on it went till they got rect.

Around end of second half, run up chip kick in air, run through defense, touched, touched, grabbed, running through 3 players chasing him, catches his own kick runs and takes it to the line. TRY.

4 points.

For a field goal to count had to get it through the basket, close but got the ring.

Kick start.

On and on till.

Houfing and puffing, B______ got the ball during a miscommunication and gave a try. TRY.

4 points.

Field goal, nothing but backboard.

Top game one that was evenly matched ."

The End

E______ "Ok, watch this boys I'm going to teach you's a new move.."

"It's called a fishie"

M____ and V___ 'A what ?'

"Just stand there and watch"

M____ 'Ok, I'm cool with that'

Reverse down the road,

Eeeeaaaaammmmmmmmmm

Winds down, out the window are you's ready ?

Small burn out, then guns it gets to our point eeeaarrrr SS eeeeeaar SS eeeeaar SS eeeeaar SS eeeaaaarr SS eeeeaaaar SS eeeaaaarr ss ss

M______ ' WOW ' did you see that

E_______ "Did you's see that ha? as his jumping out the car",

"Let me measure this one, get me a tape measure", "na, ill do feet" "This one's going to last"

M____ "That's a snake man ? why you calling it fishie ?"

"It's a fishie stupid"

The End

HAMILTON ISLAND
PEACE OF HEAVEN REAL ESTATE OR OTHER

"The first thing that comes to mind is one needs a holiday from the holiday.

From waking up at 06:00am to catch the early gorgeous cafe cater made breakfast to being on
the first Fairy to the Island.

The ride it's self, a fresh new horizon and new topography and geography, land and water, with
bright blue clear sky and bright yellow sunshine.

Eye opening, jaw dropping, natural and manmade combination of natural wonder and treasure of
Australia.

It was better than going through the gates of sesame, from memory when I did 500 years ago.
Just kidding.

The Bar had most drinks you could wish for and I chose Coke, refreshing and like the 90's
commercials I felt I was in it.

Arriving on the Island, what's so special about an island??

First things first, in this case little wise, (rather than the old, exploring blind, and explore
everything humanly possible which is fantastic nothing wrong with) we chose to look at that
map, Aha, hear, there, up, down, east, west, and explore every inch by inch.

We concluded even with our natural youthful superpowers we'd need a Buggy for this job.
And what a beautiful decision, well worth it.

All around the island we'd cruise stopping at the Gun Range, Air Glider and Beach

I even had the cocktail with the sombrero

With the closest people of my life, my brother, uncle (property guru) and myself"

The End

PIZZA AT WORK IN BETWEEN REAL ESTATE JOBS

"(A classic pizza delivery story). Wile, I finished gym and threw in the towel; I was working a night job for a while in between jobs. Pizza Delivery.

Man, the physical strenuous job of climbing stairs walking to those, too close to drive property's, streets and hills, at some points running exercise back, one two, one two use to get the, pump and fix, it was a euphoric feeling.

Reaching euphoric states at most nights as good exercise and fresh air does the job.

Even cut down on smoking through some quarters but every now and then poisoning myself with a cig, only for my body to apply adrenalin and toxic removal endorphins to further elevate my euphoria."

The End

THE SKATE BOARD

"One day, I found a skateboard 'run down and thrown out'. I put it in my car; waited till the weekend, on the weekend went to the surf dive and ski shop in east gardens asked for a repair to my trucks and wheels as those where worn out to the max and broken and they fixed it on the spot. With the coolest and most expensive trucks and wheels, custom made board, riding the skateboard was nothing short of luxury compared to my run down rusted up board I had growing up, the difference was intoxicating

So I got hooked, close deliveries where no longer a walk.. I'd jump on the board cool as Ape man the TV movie and skating I went delivering pizzas to the community.

Skating for 3, 4 hours straight!! It further pump's you up and the, focusing and balancing, further driving my uforic states."

The End

"After months and months, I was getting cocky on the board and started taking on big deliveries, competing with cars and going down, nose dive hills.

It was faster delivery's then in my car..

I swear which is why my boss was cool with it for a while; until one day I leave the board at its parking spot at the back and when I go through the back so no one sees me riding of with the board instead of walking or car, look right, look left, the board was gone.

Been busted, narrowed it down to two suspects but never confirmed the smiling crocodile.

It couldn't have happened at a better time though, as was over skating, knowing any longer I'd stack it for sure... but amazed I didn't stack it once at work while in the zone, where as use to stack it and have troubles all the time as a teenager."

The End

"(Sitting at The Park what's the best park around listening to music)

As it happened:

Long, long time ago, the silly 'Mischiefi' days, where the boundaries and limits where loose and things happened in the moment.

Different time as well; silly moments where more socially acceptable.. Now would never think off.

A 'Saturday night I believe', [it was a big get together, drinks and alcohol as much as you can drink and more, rich little crew we where, we all use to chip in $5, $10 bucks each and bobs your uncle case or two of beer.

Anyways, this night, V_______ got more pissed then me; as his little helper, he delegated his responsibility to me. After everything which is a story for another day, my mission was to take Y_______ his Girl at the time, safely home.

None the less, I was 'plasted' [drunk], as well; however the opportunity to drive the Calibra Turbo and get some 'driving experience' and 'permission' and 'gift' to drive the car made me say sure would love to..

Not knowing and minimal notice of 'not driving drunk'. 'It was always taboo as I remember, however/but I've heard of stories and people's action's made me conclude it was acceptable to be tipsy and drive'.

Never 'plasted' [drunk] but what did I know what's 'tipsy' what's 'plasted', I thought I was 'tipsy'.. Believe it or not loL.'

Happy as, but tired that's for sure ..'

Around '00:00 am' and remember as that was serious curfew for some, driving west on M4 was going fine, in a rust bucket we thought was a gem, it was a cordia turbo.

Half lost, in 'territories' out of my bounce and hating highways at the time, now love em, I managed to get Y at home..

On the way back, things got harder, [that energy of other person no longer there and lonely quite roads..

Dark, no lights, summer but [cold air night all of the sudden], freaking out if even going the right way on low to minimum petrol; I wind down the windows and pump the system loud, got annoyed by the system, I turned it off and just kept driving.

Road where getting boring and boring; eyes where getting tired and heavy as, heavy eye lids, once blinked eyes where heavier, I want to stop revive survive, but no where at the time and thought I can make it.

I drive a little more and end up in a 'dream' just from that second blink, eye's didn't open back up, just remember the dream, I must have been driving for few seconds, as only wearied off to the other side and only to be woken up by a flash of white light, bright as anything, turning a pitch black to a pitch white. I'm like talking in my sleep, what God what have I done now, only within seconds to hear a loud beep, once, twice, speaking to myself in dream state, this is not heaven this is earth, I'm driving have to wake up, only to wake up, playing chicken with a semi trailer, beep third time, with safety reflexes' going 80 or so, I get a grip and smoothly weave out in the whole moment, beeping back in thanks, freaking out and adrenalin kept me awake to the ride home..

And been the safest driver ever since.. 14 Years.]"

The End

'Had forgotten the memory, and the first memory I cherish is of older days, but a 'painting' of the tricycle I was on, (in the event and in memory banks), seen in adulthood triggered and re appeared in my mind 'fresh as the first time I was there 'yesterday', colorful and clear but mearcue and as picture, 'before my eye's', memory and made me remember it archiving it in long term memory as one of my first's.

'The first time I popped a wheely on my bike'."

The End

"With the extravagant lifestyle I would lead, taking it and pushing my limits and barriers to the limit and max all the time, came this day.

Everyday and every night, trying to reach ([euphoric] state of mind of course); however body adapts so you take it to the next level.

'What to do, that I haven't done before ?'

'The Local 'Drug Dealer' appears from around the corner; me and matey 'smile at each other', "are you up for it ? ", "yea, I'm up for it" (hmmm, that could do the trick for tonight) so we end up purchasing 4 ecstasy tablets, (thinking we will need 1 each for us and 1 each for the chicks hopefully we pick up).

Sure enough, we took one each. Blind we where, of our rocket, drinking all the while, seeing doubles at times, So we left the club and we went down to the local edge and lookout of the lagoon.

That's when we took the other one thinking will get even higher, (that's one of the dumbest things I've ever done..)

Few minutes later in conversation, I get uzzy all right, no more doubles, seeing triples and quadruples now, but what really got me scared my soul was lifting out of my body like in dreams but was wide awake.

I knew and had a feeling I was dying.

This time I didn't go to heaven or hell, but my soul and spirit lifted completely out of my body, not being able to keep my soul in body, as soon as soul detached, collapsed in coma state."

Ghost spirit hovering over the top of me seeing myself dead laying on ground, friend holding my head up, crying, screaming M wake up, wake up, M wake up, (Aaaarrrgh), to have my ghost, jump back in my body, to be suddenly woken up, to not remembering where I was, to seeing my mate relief, to being somewhat better, to saying "will never do this shit again" to telling this story."

The End

"We decided to check out a new club that just opened its doors to our home town S________ .

R_____ was the king of event planning finding new hot spots and getting puck codes from the DJ's for our free entry VIP guest lists. Incase Laki Paki and Taki were having a day off. Turned out to be a DJ too for CBD Clubs.

As it was "wow that's a big line" but fast moving, by the time we walked up everyone was walking through the doors. No VIP line that night. Strip searched top to bottom, In we go with everyone.

Ahhh, I'm with R____ who ? I'm the puck code is code .

Cool go in.

Walk through into humongous open space, with large stage and 3 slightly behind one and other (like open arena) levels of space and dance areas and couches and round club tables comfy and roomy areas. As though at the Italian forum only as a club theme at night with dim lights only packed with people dancing on the ground, stage and levels, to great sounds.

The good old days."

The End

RAVING

"I was somewhat the youngest in the clubbing crowed, (Always hanging alongside the older boys). Soon enough I came of age and the boys slowed down there clubbing nights. I had a fair bit of 'ommmf' in me left. (I started exploring field days and raves). I got tickets to a [Rave] at Sydney Olympic Park. 'This was a renowned world rate over 18's rave party'. The crowed of people that was there was more than a capacity seating crowed at a 'Grand Final Footy Game'.. The part I remember the most is from walking through the hall ways to a door way high up looking down on the floor area and around of a 'full packet out Stadium Arena', 'lights, lasers, speakers, DJ, more lights, blonds', brunette's and gush of air in my face'; looking at my brother as both our jaws dropped at the music and crowed and we both said (now that's a party)"

The End

LUCKY NIGHT

(This was a bit of panic mode night), I hadn't heard from the fellows in 'weeks', things where changing and business and takes where on the 'slump'

I got invited out to a getogether; I was sure this the night I get 'jumpt', I was being sent for.

I did my cross, sang to God and grabbed my sack of nuts and off to the party I go.

It was fight night between 'Danny Green' and 'Anthony the man Mundine'.

Man the hype was off the 'charts'; the fight was on everyone's lips that month, the bum living across the street, without TV or Internet asked me "are you watching the fight tonight". 'Should be' I say as always, (unless the latter becomes reality don't want to die as a man not of my word).

Met up with mate, things where oflly quite and sus, (I figured if I'd be dead I'd be dead by now). So he say's ' if I wanted you dead, you'd be dead by now'

Glump, glump, at least I'm not crazy I thought.

Made up on cross arguments.

So we end up at the 'Local Sports Pub'.

Packet, choka block, 'Friends', 'OG's', 'People', 'Clients' and 'Customers' all sorts from (North, From South, From East and From West); all positioned and sitting relaxed suits and ties each with their own unique trademark.

Mate, 'at ease M'.

Found our seats, relaxed and watched the beginning of the fight.

Announcements

Start

Dancing 'about', as history would tell 'knock out' in under 3 minutes, first round'.

"Yes, jump up, that's me, 'pay day', ($200 to $700.00) in under 3 minutes.

(If anyone ask's $50.00) they ask, "$700". 'Dam drinks all round'

Some 'cheering' some not we 'scatter around relaxed' socialize and celebrate for a while.

Still feeling 'lucky', and itching to play some more like everyone there, few of us went to the TAB downstairs for a punt.

$50 on Dog Number 2 as warm up,

Warm up, start, off the gates, sprint 400m

Winner Dog Number 2 '$50 to $250' Yes, got it '

Ok still 'itching', thinking (what's going on with the itch tonight???..)

$50 on Horse 7

Warm up's, 'Start', 'out the Gate', steady run with Stampede Sprint Finish.

'Again? Yes got it '

Winner Horse 'Number 7'

$50 to $200

The itch got stronger but I said that's enough for one night..

'Hung out and celebrated"

The End

CASINO

"Ha!, (another time of giving into temptation, although have repented since).

I was full of 'cash man', had 'cash coming out of my ass'; "(Petty Cash Account pocket), (The Business Account pocket), (The Savings Account pocket), (The Trust Account Pocket)" loL

Who had to do 'those one's!'; that's $10.00 for my 'right pocket', 'spending' and that's my $10.00 for my 'left pocket' emergency and not to be spent.

'Anyways', they where all topped up and had money to 'burn' for once in my life.

"(((Caught that 'carrot' been chasing for 'years', shredded it, made carrot juice, and saved up as well))"

So I go to Casino looking to make more!!, thinking back to when I use to say (if I only had money I know how to make more).

One of many as I've discovered but 'my Zaka's' was to bet safe and not worry about 'time' too much.

So I played 'Roulette' one of the maddest games out.

Had my $1000.00 playing money.

Covered 85% of the table with [85% chance to win] '($50.00 in my budget).'

[$350 on 1 in 3 chances], [$350 on 1 in 3 chance, 66% of table] and [$150 on 1/8 chance] and [$150 on 1/8 chance], [18%] of that part of table so [16% chance to lose] and {86% to win} and sure thing [I kept winning..]

[$50
$50 again
$50 again]

I'd 'pay for my lunch', 'parking' and check out a few 'chicks' at the local 'Cabaret', shout them a few drinks have a ppprrrrrrrrve as topless waitresses and 'Life' couldn't get any better, it was bliss.

Kept doing that for two, two and a bit week's day in day out.

I was making a killing a 'minca', was up [$1150 dollars], as had [lost one that kills ya..] (16% and you hit the mark as though one's jinxed).

I started getting 'greedy' like usual, (try and double your investment in the same day and do it for weeks).

'Man I was having visions of holidays, new houses, investment houses.. All it took was 5 or something years and I was set, had the plan in my head and all; as had experience in long term planning being an Agent and all, you tend to plan from time to time.
It was solid calculated budget forecast.'
Only to have a change of luck few days later..

I had reduced my capital by $650 I was now playing $350, [$125 on 1/3], [$125 on 1/3], [$50 on 1 in 8] and [$50 on $1/8] for a $50 or $25. Still covering 85% man... (That's better odds then anything I have ever been given the chance to do and succeed in man; like I'm talking... Anything, in my youth, I'd take 50% odds of achieving something and usually beat it.. 85% I never even got marks in school to that level or been in that percentile. I thought had a sure thing).

Normally I'd 'get up' a few then 'Lose' one get up again then go home.. Give or take $25 here or there to sum up to a Net of $75 to $150; playing different numbers and occasional random bet, against code; As feeling of being smart and keep things interesting, rotating my bets every now and then as playing randomly, not to raise the big brother eye or the Pit Bosses...)

They got to know me all right.. I was becoming a regular.

Until I lost on my 'first hit', then 'lost again on 2nd hit', had to dip into the 'profit' to 'lose again' and then break even, (up a little, that was break even with the labor time I put in) and with that 'stroke' of 'bad luck' kept whatever winnings I had, 'memories' and 'experiences' and got off the tables."   The End

THE BRAWLS

THE PARK

"Now this one was a crack up, OMG, it was a mad perfect night, hot, warm summer breeze and we're at nun other then the open wide green grass area of the beach, little drunk that night it was ..

I was exploring' all others representing for our County.

There would have been 5 of us Full Car, but felt like 10 of us about, so 2 Full Cars.. Pretty drunk that night so remember bits.

Out of nowhere we spot another crew, just hanging and dangling chilling off the ceilings and roof tops of the Huts.. Oh I saw them dangling about all right, got good vision I do .. In the pretty Dark Night Spot, with dark clothes, with little glows of silver belts and watches and chains, necklaces. Just sitting and laying on top.

Would have been about 5 or 10 as well another full car or two couldn't tell in the dark.

They jump down from the huts and walk towards us.

Something led to something, one guy this another guy that, there was tension over Turf if I'm not mistaken.

The Game

Anyways We decided to decide what's what over a brawl and punch up.

No Guns, No Weapons just a clean fight.

I know there were 10 as the story would tell there were about 20 people charging on the field as we were running towards each other screaming and shouting.

Anyways, Ready Steady, Set Go,

10 Wild, Crazy Faced, Men, Adults, some big, some tall, some average, some Stunning, some superhuman and huge some skinny, some Tall and Big like the one The Bravest in our crew took on.. some this that, running at us..

Us the same, wild eyed and ragged up, flexing and pumping, hot blood running through our, Veins, stretching and warming up.. All shapes and sizes, running towards them representing. Pick your person someone said, thank god, Criss crossing through the field some went, I'm running up towards the skinniest person there was, although sun of a gun was tall, he wanted to eat me alive man.. Aaaarrrgh could see his teeth they opened up and saliva running down his mouth.. He was wet at the thought of taking skinny me on..

I'm looking around for others and exits but no exits in sight... It was do or die now or never and no backing down or so I remember it.. There would have been 19 other stories of the same night, this is just how I remember it.

Bang, Wack, Pow, Wow, Smack, Crack, Asaaarough, Through, Hit, Miss, Trip, for about 15 minutes, till we ran out of steam and called a time out."

The End

SITTING AT THE PARK

"Sitting at my 'Favorite Park', 'staring, gazed' at the 'old old ancient 8 trunk body, dozens and dozens and dozens of branches' 'Tree'. (Olea Europaea Tree) I fink.

The oils produce kind of energy.

This story has happened before, but this one time, 'was vivid' and in 'deep thought'. 'Literally placing my soul and almost 'body' in a time warp window of that event in time, further criss crossing from time of event to time of event, backwards and forwards, hypothetical's to assumptions from writing on the walls to references to documentaries, helping me focus and pin point time of events as constants.
(For once the whole story came together and from bits hear bits there..)

"The Full Big Picture"

'Wow, it was amazing and mesmerizing and mearcue and heat waves'.

The Story is for you to figure out one day if you ever get the chance.

The End

CHAPTER 2 DREAMS

PART STORY PART DREAM

"Long Time ago, 18/03/06 arrived from Kuala Lumpur interchange section from Amsterdam, at Sydney.

I was in my Bedroom in E______________, centered in a 'North/West' pillow 'Head' position, always! OR 'North/East' was it LOL; to be in a position for best possible 'dreams' position, (based on Fairytales), and to get the morning sunlight based on fact and 'Solar System'.

'This day the sun did not rise in the morning or afternoon, (only realizing at 19:30 on a Saturday), after having my soul lifted so 'high up' to the 'ceiling', knowing: (once passed the ceiling, there's no way back to body as soul will not be able to pass back down the concrete, only goes up; pulled by a 'Black Mist', who's able to travel both up and down, drawing me closer and closer to his face, releasing me at the 'brink' of the 'last second' of what my 'spirit ghost' new was 'last seconds' of 'life', only for the fact, (not wanting to, but forced to) 'negotiate a deal' at that moment, that split second; only that moment, a 'calm' and 'murky and mercy' look, came over a face at back of 'Black Mist' and let me go, plunging down back in my soul, waking up gasping and gasping for air.

Light 'headache' and realizing I 'overslept' but how did I not notice the bright 'sun', I noticed every morning and afternoon.. Part of the story was in a 'pitch black' space, (like a night without any stars or moon), further woke up in a still black night.
(Instead of shaking in my boots, I put my boots back on and off to a party I went)"

The End

THE DESERT

"Man a beautiful vivid dream, (remember the last few images, wowe, 'Return' of the desert).

Walking, with an army of people, (suddenly) I'm on a camel, (I'm on a camel), but army walking alongside, (there fit and well built, thoroughbred) Horses; next to me, beside me, In front of me, behind me, about 100 people. Dressed with beautiful gowns and clothes on.

(Suddenly) Near the end and edge of a desert, not sure which desert it was but had the feel of the 'Sahara Desert', sun was yellow bit's, of bright yellow, and Hot' 'Hot', 40', 45' 'heat'. Sand was 'yellow' (sunshine and bright rich) 'sand and mountain dunes' as far as the eye could see.

(As was saying) 'Near, edge of what felt like end, we 'see' a 'Palace', (if the Taj Mahal, Best Church and Best Mosque got together, and made a Babe, White Palace type Property). (Suddenly) We get confronted by 'guards' and 'army' of 'well built men' and some 'woman' in 'well dressed' gown's.

(As said) 'After crossing, for 'days' the empty sands, with 'bit of energy', 'not exhausted' at front of, our own 'army of people'.

'No entry' was the look they gave us; so I grabbed my full bag of gold coins and 'ripped it' and through it towards them, in (rainbow triggeaction), covering the hole blue sky above with gold and gold dust and the gates of where we where 'opened'.

'The palace ended up being someone I know' further my own aunty (may she rest in peace) was sitting at the dinner table, as we once where, (back in my child hood) with somewhat (stern concerned worried but kind look) 'we where planning for lunch' (looking out the window, the hot but scary and adrenalin pumping but somehow beautiful desert) and then woke up."

The End

THE HEAVENS

"Nice dream of the 'heavens' having a chaimber room, full of files and you can select a file at will and read it; selecting a file from the clouds and researching the file.

Further dream of beautiful horse guiding me through the heavens and stars only a misty gray night with no stars in the sky, only fluffy summer night clouds. Horsey drank some water and so did I."

The End

SKY DIVE

"Dreaming of, (getting ready to skydive, preparing and getting ready from: hair to clothes to suit and safety gear, (suddenly) For split second I'm on the plain, (suddenly) free falling one third away from plain. Dropping in the air, going fast, [like 250klm an hour].

The view was amazing, (the whole world), (could see the outer shape of earth as though falling from space), colorful and bright, 'blue oceans with desert part like continents and green continents'. From looking out west to looking out to north, then east, and last south; 3D mountains and oceans, zoomed in at one then other non reactive volcanoes, the wind and speed was thrilling, the form was noise dive perfect, tightening up to catch further speed, to 'Landing' which was 'gentle dive into knee deep water' and 'Rambo roll' out.

Once out of water; (suddenly), seated dry and comfy as ever, in singlet, driving in a white 2 Door 'Jeep Vitara' through a jungle."

The End

ON THE PUNT

"Dream at the TAB, The Star City Courtyard TAB. (Couches to the east, glimmering sunshine bouncing of the water and water views to the east, sunshine bright blue sky, to the east, modern gaming machines and 'winner' music to the west, my left; as I'm standing there, 'winner' 'winner', every few seconds, 'winner, winner' but I'm focused on the beautiful, 'Spring Carnival Thoroughbred Horses Race's on the screen').

Guy I didn't recognize was there in his sharp charcoal blue, aura lit, fresh taylor made, 'new' 'alive' suit, white shirt, 'shining glimmers of light, (outlining his body and suit), wearing a gold tie, (glowing light and silver boarders around tie). 'Tall' and 'Strong', 'Godfather' type; punting away, cracking the funniest jokes, statistics on picking up again, showing, Line Graphs, Scattergrams, Charts, Bar Graphs and Pie Graphs and more, funny one's. (Must have been laughing in my dreams as woke up as though had laughed really hard).

At one point, 'trying to break through the max bet of the casino, which was $1,000,000 in my dream; a 'disagreement with management' over placing such a large bet over the limit occurred, further making me laugh out loud and that's all I remember."

The End

PAINTING DREAM

"Dream of, 'big park', modern and recently renovated; however, people/ghost standing from wile ago and at times before 1900's.

(It was more of a 'still picture/painting then a motion picture).

Over 3 to 4 Takes.

First people appeared as people playing with their kids, then they appeared as ghosts, but friendly; 5 people positioned in random order, however 4 corners, and a 5th ghost, a bit further out, with 2 little girls, playing on the swings, as I'm walking up crossing the park to get to other side.

The bit when it turned to an, 'oil on canvas painting' filled with deep dark abstract, 'dream like colours', (glowing and beating like a heart at times), was the best.

The End

THE ATM

"Nice colourful sharp very real, in the moment; eyes seeing through eyes dream of being at the ATM.

Top part poky machine, bottom part ATM. red screen, yellow outline quick tab at the button, spitting out money, $20's at first, $50's after, 'tuce' bundle thicker and thicker it got as they would dispense and fold right in my hand.

Red notes, yellow notes, green notes; (smile however feeling surprised, yes I did it). (Feelings still as though first hand; as though had figured out machine's trick to spit out money, (sweet I'm doing this to get money from now on). Eye view moving up high up to sky level looking down at myself, and checking surroundings, then zoomed right back in to eye view and bundle had a thick 'tuce' of cash at the end. Woke up to spend it, aaaahh, na na ... "

The End

THE BUS DRIVE

"Dream of, (vivid and strong) driving down a road in a coach bus (the one from the movie Speed) 'me checking for bombs and looking at brake pedal underneath making sure it works'. Over long period of time on a 'nice and neat' newly paved road, 'day and night'.

Nice friendly people on either side of me, (glamour) 'banana, sunshine blonde' joins me in conversation.

Toned, sculpted very fit guy keeps staring at me.

(Suddenly) I'm driving the bus have one other mate next to me, standing in the no standing section, smoking a cig,

Now we're back in our back row seats, 'Glamour' chatting all of us up, Ha, telling us a story' heha

I'm driving again and I tell her, we are taking her somewhere special.

Driving through a stretch of road with the most beautiful towers and buildings and apartments, city CBD residential style with Amsterdam house colors, pink, red, gray, white, purple, towers after towers, few (3 story, terraces) In-between.

I'm thinking great lots of work here, I tell them my favorite, cooperate style tower, glass panel walls, penthouse, residential apartment.

I'm still driving, headed to a special party, 3 of us, plus one more, 4th, the guy staring.

All of sudden we're on the run from police, (suddenly) on a 'country road', (Narrow and dirt on either side) the bus tips over to the left, lifting all of right side off the ground, 'crashing!!', falling 'flat on side' and 'back skidding coming to front', (creating a dust storm) 'sliding', then through a city building, (strong whiplash and 'jolt' as we 'smash through' the 'concrete wall'), smashing through 'concrete columns' then slow stop before hitting the last wall, although on a level bellow in a basement of the city building, 'choking for life', then out the bus window, breathing check, (difficult in panic mode), aiding glamour making sure she's ok, (still saying 'come with us, come with us' not giving up) , 4th guy terminator like running on the road, chasing, trying to catch up to us and fight us.

Woke up."

The End

THE DRIVE

"Before Drive at Hotel Bathroom in America, sunny hot day, brain making most similarity with California, looking out the white framed timber window in a Bubble Tiled Bathroom Wall, at one point approached by janitor, first didn't know her, was plain, then feeling of having known her, as she was busty and hot my brain is a (jump on the band wagon hootchie,) all of the sudden asking her for directions, got some direction, and off I went.

Come back half an hour later, feelings of it being the next day although same sunny day outside.

In sues way profiling checking out the Janitor to see if it's my Janitor, turns out different women, more mature Mexican Spanish, and wiser, with nice tits but everything else just average. I feel like asking her for direction, she pulls to her gold chain on her necklace and points to charm showing a red line across a weed sign, and say's we don't sell direction hear. Bit of a shock at first, but resolved tension by fluke, saying thank you politely in shock baby face style and she let me off. Tensions eased and found myself driving the car.

Driving around in a car down heading south east from west in America one of its highways, come to roundabout (realize there like us) do circle in car with female friend coco skin pony tail hair famous but didn't know which movie, now thinking back brain made most similarity with P_____ however wasn't her, something else high adrenalin happened but can't remember. "

The End

ROOF TOP

"Funny dream, (being at Sydney park), 'resolving a dispute', dressed out of uniform, in (white shoes, army pants, grey bonds, sunnies), putting it on a 'Property Manager' for all the times he's 'flexed'!!

Standing on the roof top of my building, feeling, 'finally'.

Acting and feeling like out of the Can or offset after years of mortgage, the Jeanie Bottle.

Further, dream of, 'Manager aggressively pushing me and throwing one at me, 'ducking his punch', feeling's and action and (grabbing him by the throat and arm, 'dragging' him to the edge of the wall, pushing his head over the 'balcony roof top', and saying this could be your last memory)'.

(Feelings of having to call a friend as witness to cover my alibi), although resolving it professionally and with code."

The End

 A, Tuesday 28/04/15 DE, Issue 4256,

Sydney NSW

EYES OPENED

"Cant remember dream only nice space mercury black for a while." LoL.

The End

THE NIGHT EYES OPENED

"Great vivid dream, number of low key scenarios and events.

Walking through a well established Club/Bar, 3 Females on the left, 2 on the right, 4 or 5 behind me outside the front door there was a 1 tall guy too. As I'm walking passed them; I end up in a small, 'paint peeling' light blue walls, pub/motel/hotel room. Clean but paint peeling off the walls.
Most vivid is N___ and I where just standing, long time no see greetings hugs and all, in the pub/motel, he appeared out of 'thin air' while I was just chilling there resting getting away from all the drama. After all that 'Favor' request.

Feelings of can't turn down a favor and easy one too but do my usual got to keep clean.

Then all of sudden he disappears, another guy appears, looking swave, (western oriented gentleman), (woG) but haven't met him before, confirming the request, ((I'm like who are you ?)) he's like ((you know me, don't worry..)) I'm like ((how do you know)), how did you hear ?)) ((He's like I've been doing this shit for a long time)) I'm like ((so are we going to do this or not ?)) Then he disappears into ' thin air' and comes in and appears D___ chunkier then ever before, buffed up and enforcer look type giving me clues on where I have to go..

Turns out have to take a walk through the City Centre CBD.

I'm like ((we gotta make a pinch, a black out, for a job like that)), (just to take a walk) loL loL then we were all in suits and had brief cases and we're doing the Thomas crown affair through the City CBD.

The End

THE CLIFF

"Dream of, 'was standing on the edge of a crack in the earth, on a cliff'.

(Low altitude) thinking can cross over crack with a hop step, but all of 'sudden' earth starts 'moving'; 'rising' from the earth at higher and higher altitude. (Other side of ground getting further and further away).
Working up the courage to jump anyways, all of 'sudden' (nice looking) girl chasing me from behind, (thinking insane to jump) but I 'run up' and 'jump' and fly and soared through the air. (Gliding and declining through the air for ages) then 'suddenly' Rambo turn on the ground to land safely.

DREAM LIKE THE FIRST EVER VISION

"[This is more the start of the story rather than the end of chapter], 'but sums it up too'.

'I'm little lost for words, it was a bright sunny day. It was Dad and little me, walking on 'Alexander Street', nice long residential street, suddenly out of 'thin air' appeared (future me). Not 'knowing' or 'recognizing him' at first; but the deeper I looked in his 'eyes' and 'the smile' he gave me to reassure me, I knew it was me.

(In black bonds shirt and cargo pants, standing and glowing in front of me with silver and gold aura turning into bronze glow); however had a sad look upon his face a 'heavy burden' on his shoulders. Only now 25 years later, am I able to recognize the 'face' in the 'mirror' and 'clothes and style'.

'With the worried look I gave him and the only question on my mind';

He replied "you will be all right, not to worry your life will be great, [you made it]".

The End

CHAPTER 3 BOOK FIGHT

BIRTHDAY DINNER

"It was a Saturday night, 'man Saturdays my day'.. I organized the most beautiful booking and night out.

I was cashed up that week, we booked a table at 'Quay Restaurant' I think it was, different owner back in the day and more I had a friend that worked there.

Amazing and quality design 'Restaurant' 2nd floor, window table, table with candle light for two.

No stress no responsibility, we can order anything we want from the menu.

Got the 'King Prawn's' I remember that and Hun got the 'Chicken Breast' and we ordered bits and pieces, food was delish and was sure to reach euphoria and see the lights and candles turn to murcey and as though in a Van gogh painting.

At end of dinner we had a bit of spare cash so we jumped on a 'Water Taxi' and ask to be taken for a spin around 'Darling Harbour' and back .'

Peter the Water Taxi Driver, "I'm closing up for the night, but ok sounds good, come on jump in". We went cruising in the Taxi.

Had the best night and time."

The End

"Non stop driving around 'County's and City Councils'.

We were young and surprised to even be allowed out at night! However/but we were almost adults and where allowed to drive around town on our Red P's.

Exploring for the first time.

Lights where bright, signs where glowing, ad's where making us laugh out loud, restaurants where welcoming, people where interesting, roads where fun. Those were the days."

The End

CRUISING WITH HUN

Back from a great date driving about peacefully and serene, almost home, (need to impress this chick if I'm going to get anywhere)

Driving southbound down E_______ Rd, little tipsy, gunning it, but steady measuring, calculating, speed, distance, time, triaction, and triggesction , taking probability on risk, in a lowered somewhat sports car, almost there almost there, going on energy from hear on, hun is your seat belt on, yea why, good, take it wide, rippp up the handbrake 180 through the gap in the medium strip eeeeeeeeeeeaaaaaaarrrrrrrrrrrrrrrrr on the other side almost parked..

'Wow '

Your fucking crazy" take me home now" your insane" what the fuck were you thinking" I could have died"

Ok ok, relax just a handbrake its a move you do when your a driver.

Oh, still your crazy I've had enough fun for one night" take me home"

We going there all good..

Dropped her off

'Wow that was a mad handbrake I pulled'

The End

BAR

"It was 'months and months' of clubbing and driving around and exploring new venues.

We came across a nice cozy and fancy bar, sports bar during the day, 'night club' at night.

With DJ as a 'mate of a mate' and crowed packed with familiar faces it was turning out to be a 'magical night'.

Drinks where flowing and they where 'crisp fresh'.

Amongst the hole crowed, 'choka block venue days with crowed capacity at peaks', I layed eye's on the prettiest girl just dancing with another friend, little board.

I swear that's like the 3rd time I have seen a 'glimmer'. Mirage and time wrap vortexe hole around the presence of her body and then a little image in my head crystal clear of us two holding hands in a field watching our kids play.

'That 3rd time was the time I started trusting my sixth sense and gut feelings although never really talking about it much till now obviously'.

Sure enough, I introduced myself and started dancing with her. 8's and circles even around her... As I'm twirling her as her turn to do 8's, I close with the tight hips and close face to face energy charge only to ask her to hang out with me for a while.

Excited she said yes, I lost track of all other things that night just focused on getting her name and number.

Somehow she did just that and we danced and hung out all night, amongst a crowed of friends acting like I hardly know anyone lol.

Months and Months of 'Bliss' thereafter."

The End

'FIRST NATURAL DISASTER

Out of nowhere after months and months of good times there was a change of wind and I had come to a point of outgrowing my relationship or actually being too immature for it and things went sideways and on each other's own."

The End

FIRST TIME SINGLE FOR A WILE

Life was slower, clouds where darker, sky was darker; everything in my body was heavier, things where boring but I applied some self preservation techniques and bounced back."

The End

"After settling and slowing down I was 'pozzessed' by a book Hun had in her collection. Knowing: the way to a woman's/man's heart is through there stomach, "however/but knowing what they've read can help; to get in their dreams".

So possessed as I was to explore the mind of hun in detail, and losing all focus and attention on reality and 'hun' her self, deeper and deeper into the book I went, reading page for page, just about to 'climax' in satisfaction at the last 40 pages of 200 plus, she jumps at me, that's enough, give me that, that's mine, you can't have this, let go. No you let go, no you let go, no get off me , get off me, rolling around, from funny, getting heated, to neither of us letting go, to her finally ripping it out of 'spite' and me letting go not to rip it further and losing the battle .. Dying to read the 'End' I ask for it back, just give it back, "Noe", "Noe".

Kissed and made up; that 'settled' her."

The End

THE BAR NIGHT

"Woo hoo a night for the 'books' alright, after hours and hours of sipping drinks, mate working all night, it was closing time.

"Last Drinks, Everyone out".

All the locals started leaving but nun of the regulars felt like budging that night.

'Stinking Hot Summer Night'.

"Right, since you's aren't leaving I'm locking you's in".

'Closed Bar, Night Out'!!!

Cold Beers poring all night..., (at times pouring your own beer, a first for me after so many many schooners, [It was a new schooner experience]).

Topless Table Dancers, 'ok not all completely topless, but some', short skirts as well; completely see everything under skirt as they through their legs in the air, compliments of the Females.

Partied till early sunrise 6am in the morning."

The End

THE POOL PARTY

"We finally had organized a 'group getogether' of; couple's, single's, neighbors and other to the classy, 1000 Unit, Arena Style Complex 'pool'.

From, nose dives, to bombs, to feet first, to summersaults to back flips to sideways we kept jumping in and out of the water in the perfect hot day."

The End

ROOF TOP

"Roof tops were my fave thing, being a cat and all loL.

Prrrrrrrrrr as I was looking for the next rooftop I haven't been on.

Turns out, shopping centers have rooftops, (however nothing like 'Residential Buildings' and 'Towers' as stories will tell).

We had coffee, It was the 'Car Park' and we walked to all four sides to check out the views.

Nice lookout's".

The End

"Oh man this was a mad day. It was a Saturday and on top. Hun and I had jack to do.

We had talked about visiting the centerpoint lookout, however put it in the we'll do it yednoh lepah dana, 'one beautiful day', "but after 20 years of waiting for that beautiful day, you find out the ending to that saying, your family dropped it on ya(one), after 20 years of hope that beautiful day will come, but maybe never".

Anyways back to the story we caught that beautiful day and we were at centerpoint.

Top of the what use to be tallest building with 360' uninterrupted views of the neighborhood and hanging there with hun.

Nothing really exciting happens in this story, it was just a mad date."

The End

LUNA PARK

"Woohoo

"Train to Circler Quay, 'Fairy Ride', "love the ride", there the best ! Use to get them from here to Parra to Manly and back.

(This book will never fly overseas will it; is there a point describing a ferry ride experience, we all know the ride however hear goes).

It's a two story motor powered boat, aka Fairy. With a [bow], "front I think", a [stern] back I think, a yak and a [wak], "(Stafford and Port)"

Nicest thing it's got the seats outside in full circuit. 'I've made sure I've sat at every possible angle', cause that's the type of son of a gun I am loL. Do things till its soar loL,

But my fave is the bow and stern of Fairy!

On a windy and rocky day, you get splashed with water; on sunny and smooth day it's just mad watching the whitewash!!

So as where going across the Harbor to save, "1 hour drive through traffic and roads", on this trip, we're there in 10 minutes.

Hop on, 'few minutes ride' hop off.

'See you later, alligator' !! .

Walking through the mad 'Mouth Clown' is the best ride; there after it's even better!!

It's been years since I stepped foot in this state of the art 'Amusement Park'.

Lights, music, scenery, rides, food, it has it all.

We got a couple of tickets, (not the usual as kids, jump on every ride at every different angle just because) but a couple of good safe fun rides.

We chose the 'Ferris Wheel' and the 'Mini roller coaster ride'. I forgot the name, I'm old now loL, "I remembered it for years but writers block at moment".

Ferris Wheel, as they go, you wait in line, all the time looking at the wheel spinning all the while thinking (hope they don't get stuck up there or injured),
(all the while, 'geeing' yourself up for the ride)
(If I go on, it's just my luck I bet it will freeze on me).
(Worried not for the fact someone may injure them selves but you'll lose your turn on the ride)

It's our turn and we get settled.

Slowly rising, 12' by 12' as everyone in line gets a chance to settle.

Finally you get to the top; unlike anything in the world, (as unique in itself), the 'rich' and 'beautiful' up close and personal Sydney Harbour Bridge. 'Beautiful panoramic views' of the 'tip and coast line of the city fringe', deep blue water's, on either side as far as the eye's could see, surrounded by water front, concrete jungle developments, last but not least, 'Fairy', 'Boat's' and 'Water Taxi's' zooming passed, under the massive and amazing Sydney Harbour Bridge. Its just as it sounds, you feel as though your on a beautiful swing high up swinging of the Harbour Bridge.

(Your saying freeze, freeze), let me stay up here for a little while longer as your looking out to the panoramic view.

'Round and Round' smooth and nice around the Wheel we go, where will stop nobody knows.

The Modern Mini Rollercoaster, was fast as, faster then I remember it as a kid.

Cool Rides."

The End

"One or few like 100 dates of dinners and cafe's, coffee's and 'silver platters'; top notch cafe's, restaurant's, bar's and venue's.

The best, 'self praised', world 'Renowned' cook, keeps asking to go out on dinner dates."

The End

THE JAQUIZY

"The one I fever the most; "is our time at what we found; after years of daydreaming about, only to sit down one day with the cash to do it, is to relax together at the 'Jacuzzi Natural Therapy'.

We would have called 15 to 30 Hotels looking for a room with a Spa or Jacuzzi.

The usual responses No!. Yes; but, bath tub spa's, "no thanks", yes, however there $1000, a night "no thanks", yes, but there booked!! Yes, but only one and you have to make appointment.., $400 a night, fair enough, almost did it if it wasn't for my double check, 'No thanks'.

Hit the jackpot and thank god for S_____S____ and Natural Energy Jacuzzi's."

The End

THE BOAT CRUISE

"It was Australia Day 'long weekend', we booked a 'Dinner Cruise'

Cruizing around the Harbour.

Picture Perfect, nice chicken dinner, nice night, warm cool breeze, stars in the sky, at the bow,
Titanic Style."

The End

FAVE POAM

"Roses are Red, violets are blue, I'm in love with you."

The End

"On a faded fortnight and month, with having worked and trained and studied, the luck of catching a wink in 'peace'; thinking blissfully would together fall asleep in the night.

I ask for a glass of water, simple water, as thirsty from gym, to recharge and rejuvenate a little. Only to get a 'spiked', glass of water, not knowing sculling it straight as you do with water, "Oh not so fast hun", "it's ok it's water", 'aha' only for minutes later to be charged up, complete opposite of what was meditated and planned for to get a high but almost heart attack at same time.

For some reason that's the last time I'm confessing to a supposed pass on sex to hun."

The End

MY JOURNEY BEGINS AT NHSPA

"Hear we are, NHSPA, I've mentioned a story one in the other story's however it can't be left unsaid (as my all to well friends keep reminding me) "(Goes without saying)" you hear that in this neighborhood.. However it started by nurture and care rather than nature or was it VISE versa. A place to nurture and develop your creative side, from small things big things grow, what I'm trying to say is from a small idea sprung from a class exercise, worked on it worked on it for years and years, guided and taught, experimenting and researching as needed research and experience, so to, sais I, started plotting and weaving it, pushing my limits with experiments and research, built on it, risking my ass at times, to developing it into a book. Maybe I should have added my all too favorite high school stories however that's a book on its own and Episode I .

Just a little shout out and credits to the Team."

Mwwwwaaa L all, yea I sort of don't do that anymore as the story's will tell.

The End

"It was a (Beautiful Bright Sunny Day), but we didn't know it, as we were on the 3rd floor of a classroom with our backs to the window.'For good reasons, otherwise easy to daydream out the window, I can attest too'.

(It was an honor and dream being in that Tafe), anyways the class was so so 'that day', interesting and informative, days it's mind blowing are cool".

BBBRRRRRRRIIIINNNNNG

BBBBRRRRRRRRRRRIIIIINNNNNNNGG

BBBBRRRRRRRRRRRRRIIIIIIIINNNNNNG

'What's going on, did class finish early ?

Teachers saying, "It's the fire alarm in orderly fashion exit the building".

'For some reason I thought it was a real one'.

(I've been in Fire Alarm Test's before but I thought it's a real one that day)

I was outside, a fresh breath of fresh air and I was calm. (The Gush of Wind)

Now this next bit is a paradox, what was then was to be was now was then to be.

A small world we lived in.

The thing I remember is this one Guy rounded us up in a group, lined us up in rows; (in a group like troops from an army) and asked us questions on Real Estate.

"Who will help me manage my units ?"

Off the bat, (I was quick off the mark back then); (at the back, in last row with the tallest and 'Giants', however the smallest and skinniest as late bloomer in life)

Raise my hand.. "You come hear"

Walk through to the front, "I know this area like the back of my hand, I can help you manage".

(One looks at me he said that's good but your too young and threw me back in the crowed).

The Question I've always had is what pulled him and urged him on that day, that hour, that minute to act out possessed as not the type to pull pranks like that.

The End.

NEW MANAGEMENT

Early morning that day up with the 'Kookaburras' .

Sun is rising clearing the night, 'sourcing your energy', feeling it and knowing today's going to be a good day.

Preparation to even 'Rehearsal' of your magic tricks and files in suit case, and on your laptop.

Looking like a shining new penny from top to bottom.

Hair done good, kornjacha shirt, 'Kelly Country Suit, matching jacket and pants 'thank god', fresh $90.00 tie and shining newish Colorado shoes.

Pen and 'folder', empty with bit of paper; in case you need to hit someone over the head with.

Mental check, 'reports and statistics' 2nd check in head, warm up to 'Personal Quote' and off you go to the first shop that comes to mind.

Background check.

"'Follow up's', 'Walk inn's', or 'Referral' or 'Other'

-Name

-ph

-Property Address

Put together a file

- Inspection

- Appraisal Letter

- Comparable

- Agency Agreement

- Other

Property

Unit/ Apartment/Lot /Block, Tower, Complex

Semidetached House

Federation, Californian Bungalow

Spanish Mission, Liner Style Art Deco

Post War Weatherboard

Contemporary 50's, 60's, 70's 80's 90's 21st century. Free standing Eclectic

Federation Revival, Resort Style, Environmental, Victorian Terrace

and

'Other'

a) Knowledge & Hard Yakka

b) Conduct

c) Security

d) Act

e) Regulations

f) Finance

g) Keys

h) Other

Security Key ONE END

Front Door Key

Room Keys OTHER END

Window Key

Carapace Garage Key THIRD END

Usual places office, at property or at client's office or property, occasional cafe to sign.

The Hard Lease/ Management / Most Likely

The Average Lease/Management / Most Likely

The Easy Lease/Management/ Not likely

'Other'

On and on it goes, like mail it never stops coming." LoL to the bank.

The End

"Once apon a time in the days of K____ X____ , I was given instructions to replace the 'blinds' in a (studio property).

10 Step manuvers.

'All the wile praying for a receptionist that has a clue..'

At appointment, (blinds hanging by a thread...)

Tradesman 'woom' pulls down on blinds the 'hole rack' falls down.

"Mate these defiantly need replacing" although I'l put them in my truck may use them as second hand"

"But occupier needs Blinds wile we're in the process of repairing "

"I don't know about that but I'm taking these as insurance, I didn't come out hear to quote for nothing"

As blinds all ready 'cactus' no need to 'give him the '303' and 're fit blinds', as getting replaced with new one's (or second hand repaired one's by sound of things)

Get 'quotes', 'forward' to owner for approval.

Wait day or two to hear back, 'P and R' with owner, (Boss kept saying it, till this day don't know what that stands for but I figured, report things to owner')

The End

ARREARS

"The usual 'smooth operator' that sneaks through the 'system',

First 3 months all good then the 'dramas' start.

'Phone call' followed by a 'letter'.

'No Reply'

'Phone call' 'msg' 'email' followed by a 'letter'.

"Il pay just waits till tomorrow"

'Phone call', 'msg' followed by 'letter'.

'Other'

"Il pay just something came up sure thing in 3 days"

'Diaries'

'Phone call', 'msg' followed by letter.

"I don't have the money but I'll get it in 5 days"

'Diaries'

'Phone call' 'msg' followed up by 'letter' followed up by written 'payment plan'

'Other'

This goes on for 2 or (other) months then he slips up to the point of being 14 days plus late.

At 15th Day

Phone Call and 'Notice Letter' or

'Other'

"Upgrade 'security' incase of 'backlash'"

No reply, no reply, (by now his playing the 'game' of why communicate with you .

(Payment options provided) or

'Other'

(Physical inspection of property as may have abandoned property; still living there, finally chance to confirm when he'll be coming in to pay some rent)

"Tomorrow for sure".

'Diaries and follow up' or

'Other'

Made half the payment, back to the drawing board from step one.

Or (Other) under new school

On and on it goes, however taking this direction.

Lodgment of application to Tribunal, complete file 'double check' and present.

Appointments and updates to landlords and Bosses and Further Confirmations, check.

(Wait another 7 to 14 days for a hearing and present case praying to god you haven't made a typo as its back to the drawing board) or 'Other'

'Finally order for the boot'.

From hear there are a few options and courses that can take place.

One course; not the worst; At order for the boot, (forward copy of order and present to Occupier).

Depending on X___ factors assessing your action plan.

"Physical inspection to check if occupier vacated as per orders, praying left and clean or abandoned even, you can move on"

You find out 'abandoned all right', (asking God why abandoned why abandoned), (shit left everywhere, messy and unclean.

Double check with Occupier picks up saying all rubbish claim it from the bond.

Bond covers the rent and $B for clean but job is $D

'Negotiations on the phone'.

'Insurance Claim'

Lodge bond claim and organize clean and repairs.

'List' property back on 'market' and 'take' 'unapproved', 'half a day off' to 'unwind' and 'breath' [happy as] thanking God at least you weren't (shot at today).

Or 'Other'

And having to do it again the next day for another 5 Occupiers."

The End

OUTGOING BOND INSPECTION

"Notice to 'Vacate' received.

(Chance to get paid or lost your time and money (you'l never get back) and lovely warning your out of a job in 14 days as you haven't leased it on the day, or Other .

One 'replies' and forwards the appropriate letters.

Set up appointments for outgoing.

At outgoing with complete file and bond claim form.

Double check, approx 400 x or tick tabs, plus overview, plus clean, plus double check keys.

Other, Excellent, Satisfactory, Very Good, or usual 'Something's not right', (Negotiations and dealing with conflict)

Explain the 'outstanding rent' and 'carpet stain' not noted on 'pictures and condition report'.

"But it wasn't us, it was there to begin with"

(In this case).

Double checking file again to make sure as always gave benefit of the doubt.

"As you can see, not on Pictures"

'Ok we can afford half the cost for repair'

"We need the full cost of repair.."

'Apply' tradesman quoting techniques to resolve dilemma and negotiate.

Few options from hear; conflict can reach agreement or it can turn into a full blast tribunal case.

In this case, closed with will get the quote and advise you then.

Obtain quotes, (a full time job on its own).

This Person gets their own advice, once settled, time and date and place for signing of Bond Claim Form.

Or Other. Hearing at the Tribunal

WORKING

"Working nothing but working for 2 years"

The End

"Working some more and then working nothing but working"

The End

BOUGHT A UNIT OLALA

"It was after '6 years' of 'on and off work' through '3' different jobs; I saved up to be comfortable enough to trust myself. To have the knowledge and know how, (what was somewhat thinking back now), [knowing what I know now]; as being in the property game, was to except the gift from my parents and invest in a property of my own.

After (years and 6 months) of research for an apartment or house, (which was life changing commitment) I decided to do the open house inspections.

With 'international' open house experience; 'Laws', 'Rule's, 'Code's and 'Lifestyles' we narrowed it down to one.

That one turned out to be a winner."

The End

THE GYM

"Best times ever, together sneaking into 'our own Private Gym' (sneaking in, as worried may get pulled up on having brought more than one mate).

'First it was one on one, then three, then five, before we knew it, there was 7 of us, (where all working out and training hard)'."

"While working 7am to 7pm, the only money I had left after (mortgage repayments and bills) was very little, $100 to $150 a week.

(So 'being able' to do 'nothing', (as anything I did required big capital, didn't know better) further little window of time to spend, (before have to rest for the next day work); I had further invested in my personal development growth. 'Training at the Gym with the Boys'.

'It started with light exercises and just being 'euphoric' at the fact had my own personal state of the art 'Private Gym'.

'Before I knew it (within 3 months of training, I felt growth in muscle, tone and pump). Pushing each day little more and each day to the max and feeling fantastic; Percolating after each work out.

(After a year and a half or so I started managing my properties verbally and not having to use that much supporting documents). LoL.

'Soon I started growing muscle weekly, getting thicker and thicker; However drama with my loved one, got me upset and depressed; no time for gym, losing the years and months momentum I had built up'.

The End

THE GYM

"(Few times there'd be [chicks]).

'Well this time I had my game on, fuck the training, LOL.

I start 'tuning up' and the usual questions rolling off my tongue as second nature as experienced in dealing with people by this stage,

"Who ever loved that not loved at first sight"

One smooth line, after another, crack of a joke, after another, after the other, had the girl smiling all right.. (So we exchanged numbers).

(Hot and steamy as she was, riding her steps, in tights, [box showing] I wanted to take her on the spot in front of the hole gym).

But obviously was civil about it and did our fair wells to catch up another time.

That 'same night', ring ring, ring ring, I'm home alone, want to come over for a pizza and a movie...

'Il be there in 10min'

The End

EARLY MORNING DRIVES

"Now that I was a home owner it was a different ball game altogether.

'Skating on thin ice (however doing figurines and 8's) thin ice as only as good as my last week's work performance review.

Ice skater (ole)

Had to 'minimize risk' as had a 'large bond' as 'deposit'. 'One' sudden mishap, 'hospital' or 'jail' or 'big fine' or (murder) would have set me right back.

However, I had the luxury of observing the night life early in the mornings going to work.

I would get up at like '06:00' in the morning and 'go towards work' (which was a 25min drive); do 'happy laps' around the 'X' looking for leftovers from the night before.

So often there would be a nice girl I would chat up, the complimentary flash, but nothing more than that, the area was also like an office type and still had mad respect for the office.

But it was 'fun' seeing alcho's, strippers, and all types from time to time around the area." LoL.

The End

OFFICE KEY

"The 'Time and Day' I ([quick stick], stick in the sand); grabbed the key off my bosses 'hand'.'It was an afterhour's afternoon, after months and months, 6 months; felt like 12 months. The day came when N___ was getting tired of staying back and monitoring our early morning starts and late night finishes. (To my advantage that was, now I remember was working on that...)

Anyways it was senior property manager and junior property officer me.

As was saying late in the afternoon, after hours of months and months of productive good work.

N____ decides to 'reward' us as he so often does gotta say.. (However he was doubtful on my age I felt.)

'He pulls out a key, holds it in the middle, 'both' of us jaw drop't, [AWaah], standing still for 5 seconds, processing the 'beauty's and wonders' of having our own key; then leaning towards giving it to senior manager, 'Mate 1, P______ the maddest property manager ever, as he must have seen me 'drawling', but 'snap out', quick came in the 'hand' as Mate 1 (jaw was still dropping), 'snatch went the reflex' faster than light, no time or vision to even [slow mo the scene] or even tighten his grip as we [slow moe once seeing something fast, at eye level] from hand reach distance 'He didn't see that one'.

(Hand was quicker than the eye that day)

Right in the pocket, 'what happened ?'

'And with that, risky I hear ya, however so was reassured and awarded a key to keep. Mate 1 got one too, next day'."

The End

A GOOD DAY

"It was a busy Saturday night, (by this time I had shaped up and was a mature adult, beyond my years).

All was going smooth and had not done a mischiefy thing for years and years, '18 to 27, 9 years' solid stand up guy.

It was before the new laws, (for no phone while driving) where introduced, as far as I known about it; I developed a bad habit. Business man and all, would get calls in the toilet, let alone driving from point to point.

The new laws took effect or at least I heard they were in forcing them, 'man was spewing' however the law is the law, must obey the law, as was integrated in my upbringing; and mother lawyer background.

Anyways I ended up having to take a 'very important call that night', I was, on the phone talking, 'stopped' 'not driving', (car on, standing) and in quite back street, no one can see me.

Vooom, drives passed the life shaking, brand new, 'shinning', 'police car', (jam packet, 5 in the car if not 7 from the look of things), [buffed up Agents]. You could tell they were more Agents, then just officers.

[Point Blank, Gun in the Face]

I was a 'goner', last few points, but had a few; jaw dropped, almost heart attack, they unloaded and off they went.

OMG, God blessed me that day.

No ticket for once, [got $30,000] in credit with the SDRO in support."

The End

FIRST LEASE

"My job was [do as I'm told]; after my whole 'education', 'knowledge' and 'training' was defiantly reconfirmed and assured [I know jack].

Very friendly and open arms welcome by N______ (anonymous for this book, as we value our privacy) and finally found a place I could 'rest a little' in a small business, after studying and working in large company's over '200 employees' for [2 Years], night shifts and studying day shifts; story for another chapter.

As was [do as I'm told] further reading my 'notes from Tafe', trying to 'interpret the law' to give me 'insight' and 'better understand of the game', (to better do as I'm told), as it's: 'Address and mission in this game'... One has to 'know', 'what steps to take' not to get 'burnt...'

With my 'me-giver moves, at the 'time' 'downloading from Internet', when hardly anyone had the Internet, '[before, 'Google' I believe], not sharing, (trying to outsmart the boss), develop ways to communicate better'; I started reading the 'Act' for real, not as an assignment. (On the job, as you know who would attest too, 'he was always reading..'

Finding, what I needed to find to put elegant pressure in my favor; the new legislation and Act, against normal 'old school trade practices' was to 'always' 'at all times' inspect a listed property with the 'company of an Agent...'

Not as 'quoted' in 'act' but along those lines as little worn out from formalities and in creative writing. [Not like me].

'Oppose to the old school key deposit, you give ID and $50 or $100 and hears the key, you maybe familiar with'.

['I was sure to point that out, to keep my job, as could be replaced with simple two min conversation. (Silly me at the time.. thinking now, I thought I knew something, 'Rocky thing' but penny drop't later in experience.
'Personal Vent']

'Off the start, in the 'deep waters', in a day or so; was given the mission to lease (a mortgaged out to the teeth) 'vacant, empty, for two weeks now', repossessing pressure breathing down my neck, swave', but more than 'swave', ' stylish' and 'super studio' not knowing at the time.

(Taking a breather at this age from the young day's pressure.)

'Looking good!!' 'Fresh as a [daisy]' with (somewhat knowledge of the 'Leasing Consultancy, Property Management and Real Estate Game) on time with 'Keys and Forms and Brochures' to 'guide me' and improvise as I go.

Anyways the physical '2-1/2 K ' walk to unit was a breeze as was light and bouncing on my feet.

(As though {the wind beneath me} as the saying goes..)

On 'time', 'standard' meet and greet.

Walk through the whole building as my style; take them through every point... 'car space', 'security hall ways and lift's', 'level' 'Roof Top'; (oooh, and what a gorgeous roof top it was, {to die for}, looking out to 'Rushcutters Bay'. 'Marina, Boats, and Green Grass' on a sunny, 'bright blue day'), then apartment studio, through the usual layout in some order.

[Serious moment as eyes locked and tenant was interested].

'Outlined the 'lease' and notes, with little known meaning behind the application form, 'lease' and 'condition report', as was my style; present, inform, prove and explain.

[I managed to receive an application form for processing.]

'Wooo weeee'

'Got a pat on the back and job well done'

(At that time that was all thank god, only if I knew I've got a tone of work to look forward too).

The End

"Once I got: confident and more confident; I was starting to get valuable advice, (some general advice and tips some more advanced).

The evident try and show as many properties as possible, taking 3 sets to 5 sets of keys, doing private open's to 5 properties, 5 different buildings, 5 different addresses, some different council but many subtle and major differences, in under 45 minutes.

'It wasn't good enough, 'verbal and written paperwork' one had to go out and physically show and open one's eyes to the advice.

5 properties 'an' inspection, 15 properties, '15' different addresses, ' a day'

On and on it went till I got a firm grip of the 'styles and faults'

'Management was crucial'

One after the other after the other, I leased them all!! But one! From, 18 Vacant Units, to 1 remaining on the list.

Wanted to write 'SOLD OUT' that month, and go on a mini holidays for a 'Week', but New Managements and Referrals Just kept coming in.

Of course I'll take new managements I'm not saying don't give me new managements so I can go on holidays just one vent that month. If you ever find my office.

The End

TWO HOTTIES

"It's a major difference to how it was and how it is, the story I'm trying to tell is the one or two times before (my good old society and generation decided to upgrade to new and improved systems).

The days where, listings where listed for sale prier to 'contracts being drawn up'; the days open house inspections were carried out with 'key deposits', more to the point making me laugh is the 'key deposits' .

In walks in the 'local corner girl' to inspect the 'same' vacant property for the 5th time this week.

"Hi, I'd like to place a $100.00 refundable key deposit for the studio on M_______ St, I'll be back in 30min".

"Sure, hear you go... 'Receipt' and No smoking in the units or clean up after your self and turn the lights off and close the windows".

(I was like at least she's thorough in her inspections).

'1 hour goes passed, no key returned, 2 hours go passed, no call or return'

Call the mobile to follow up; as have inspection to carry out with owners, no answer.

Ok ok, cool down been in stickier situations before.

Jump in the 'bat mobile', as fuck walking around those days.. Drive down and park.

Spare keys in hand, up the stairs, 'open the doors to inspect its presentable for owner more than anything'; two females, a Hotty and a Hotty, getting it on; on the floor. loL.

(OMG)

"Hey, knees a little weakened, (fuck if only I had more time), 'man up', hey, shows over, get dressed, we gotta get out of here, landlords coming to inspect in 30 minutes, chop chop, snap out of it".

"Ok ok, you don't have to be such a prick about it.."

All dressed, cleaned up and presentable off we went.

Owner inspects; smells like badussy in hear, 'pussy, ass and dick', where did the $100 go.

The End

THE BLACK FERARI

"Driving 'out of nowhere', actually coming from East, driving West, 'passed 'our' street' was the black, '355 model', 'new' Ferrari.

With the new Star 17' rims, stock body, with custom exhaust and yellow badge logo.

See's me 'staring' and 'slows down', wind's window down and say's "would you like to take it for a spin around the block" ok he said "would you like to go for a spin around the block"

(Nice looking clean gentleman), "Cool, 'yeas' sure thing"; "Jump in" and around the block we went. "

Mad Ride.

The End

RED FERARI

"Once upon a time, early days, I was coming back from an inspection, hot sunny day, was taking a breather.

Just outside our office/shop drove past a 'Beauty' old school red Ferrari.

"I'm looking for a property can you help me out?"

Dodgy looking character, (scared to jump in, even me); It was the X. Not my first time scared to jump in, or a sudden character following you.

I work up the courage, (what the hell if I die today, I've lived a good life).

'Sure I'll jump in, wear we going?'

"Just taking you for a drive around the block; wile you tell me what properties you have on your books"

(It was bogus appointment, but I took it, get out of office a little more). LoL.

I open my folder, qualify and go through the list of available properties... The spill.

He takes me too, 'Victoria St'.

I'm like 'why we stopping?'

Have a look at this, showed me a pic of a naked chick and then chicks on his phone.

'Hmmm' composed.. As I wasn't all that impressed knowing 'Bigger and Better' seeing much better.

I said cool.. why you showing me this ?

"How would you like a taste".

Thoughts of (starting up a side business and accepting the offer; rising through the underbelly went through my mind. However I held out for the bigger boss.

'No thanks I said'."

The End.

THE POINT I STARTED TWO BOOKS

"The thought of (being amongst the PIMPS AND PLAYERS got me thinking).

(I was defiantly young dum and full of come).

I let temptation get to me.

For '3 months' I would work 'extra hard', earlier starts and later finishes working till 9pm sometimes '11pm' all in efforts to find end seduce a more appropriate 'applicant' for my 'vacant' units.

At one point had 3 levels, 'that's 24 units', (with all criteria and qualifications, further passing all landlords criteria; coincidently the 'Hottest of Hot', young and fertile Male's and 'Females').

It was moments before I started handing out flyers, (welcome, welcome, this type, that type, all type, hear at Mexico LOL LOL); only to come to my senses scrap the hole plan; even though 'females' and 'males' committee 'we created' were hoping for and counting on client tell.

Closest I became to having a side business."

The End

THE DRAGON

"The 'Day's' where improving going from 'good' to 'fine' to 'perfect days'.

The funny thing was, I was getting séances I never knew I had.

One time it was early morning my smell was so acute I smelt the perfume on a girl from her being 150 yards away. loL.

My mind was sharp and organized thoughts where crystal clear.

I was standing next to my mate and over his shoulder above in the sky I saw my 5th vision.

An 'Orange Dragon Appearing'; (ripping out from the air under the blue in the sky, as though squeezing through an elastic hole in the air, (2000 feet altitude)

Flapping its wings, 'fire orange in colour', (like Phoenix); within seconds forming and being more from this universe. (At one point exactly like the main 'Dragon' in 'Avatar' the movie, except way before the movie came out).

(My 'Feelings' overdrive, overwhelmed, although did my best to channel them).

My first thoughts we're, (as though from a 'parallel universe' of the 'same area'). The feelings grew and changed, tapped in and were closer and more in tune with as though from the 'passed', while I was receiving a picturing as clear as day in my mind of the hole Jurassic Park. Jurassic Environment of the X.

The pterodactyl's and Dragons flying playfully together in the sky 7 throughout the area of City of Sydney and few four legged and long necked land dinosaurs. (Diplodocus/Brachiosaurus)

The X as a Jurassic Park.

Passed that vision further staring into the 'Dragon', its 'alive' as though from our time a séance he knows and it's comfortable with its surroundings.

"Heard the screech of her roar too"

Seconds later laying a golden egg at the beautiful (cul-de-sac of the natural beauty of Elizabeth Bay) and just above the 'Onslow House'."

The End

COMPUTERS

"The time and day (I caught up with my work and had time to spare). After months and months of exciting, however hard work, I took advantage of the fact I had keys to the office.

Everyone left for the afternoon and so they said 'you sure you want to stay'.

'I'm sure need to catch up on some work'.

Gliding walks passed a glamour yet again, (there's a few in Sydney).

'Nice Legs', 'thongs', 'yellow shorts', 'singlet t-shirt', didn't do anything, just ran up to the door, said 'hi' and she said 'hi' back. Wanted to invite her in but had too much respect for my work place; 'there was a basement, thinking now', but the dream was on the desk.

Anyways missed out.. That time. LoL.

Jumped on computer surf through some 'X rated pictures and films, I hear a pop, the computer goes black with a white line closing to a dot.

I said I've done it now; although that was my first real honest 'my' mistake after 2 years.

I believe I had some credit, was in shock but relieved a little back up was done and the computers where old /ancient and N_____ all ready planning to replace anyways.

Knowing about computers somewhat new that was it for that one.

Tried restarting but 'Caput'.

Still keen and in 'doubt' it was my error thinking (coincidence as other coligue, showed me a file that worked on his computer but 1 months ago).

So I jump on coligues computer tried downloading and 'pop again'.

I'm freaking out, (what kind of jinks is this), although (thanking God computers ancient), even 'I' could afford to replace them as my motto agreement was.

I break I pay.

Next day, we ordered new computers, top notch; was looking forward to using them."

The End

THE BALCONY

It was (6 to 9 months) in my role as property officer.

I received an 'invitation' from mate to join him in an open house, of a 'Newly', 'Brand Spanking', 'Just Completed', 'Actual, 21st Century Development' and apartment for sale.

Wowe, 'it was elegant', a rare development, from the 'outside' it looked 'fantastic' but from inside was 'marvelous'.

The architecture was such that it took my mind to a major Titanic/ Oceania Cruise Ship / 'like ship'.

Exceptional external finishes and internal finishes.

We walked to the '7th Floor' I believe, one of the 'penthouses'.

The design was open plan, spacious and airy, (a light lift of spirit as you walking in and through the front door). The finishes where brand new.

I was invited further more to inspect the balcony.

This is when I literally 'froze', tightening of each muscle in body, ' 'Uckochen'

Eye's automatically adjusted, I did nothing but stare for 5 minutes, jaw dropped, 'Aaaah' suddenly feeling the gush of fresh air as it went running through my face.

Uninterrupted, ('The City Night Sky Line of Sydney Australia, in one of its best forms; Walt Disney Picture and Night).

A view as far as the eyes could see.

I was literally snapped out and was told it's time to go.

[2.5 Million] at the Time."

The End

ROOF TOP 1

"The most humble to me 'Roof Top' would have to be the one at: X marks the spot.

It is the '8th Floor' of a '4 Tower Complex' in Pyrmont overlooking Darling Harbour.

Strong and stable, modern and new, tiled and clean, little benches to sit on and chairs around, with nice glimpses of views.

The 'Best' thing is the most gorgeous lovely 'Fruit Bearing Lemmon Tree'."

The End

ROOF TOP 2

"The 'Roof Top' of a small 'Art Deco' Building.

Facing West/North/East/South

Positioning on the edge of a Hill / Point of X______

Roof Top, 'Garden/Terrace' with timber picnic tables.
Strong and stable, reinforced concrete frame, brick exterior, with pebble stone tiles as floor to Roof Top; 270' of uninterrupted serene and tranquil, city skyline view.
So much sky above and uninterrupted you can see the hemisphere, city CBD skyline 'buildings' and fresh healthy green valley type grass 'Domain Park' to feed the eye's, as though our city skyline is in a garden of eve.

Busted a lady sun baking topless and in a G-String one Saturday morning."

The End

"The 17th Floor of a Residential sky scraper Tower.

Harry Sadler Architecture, on prime location and Cul-de-sac Street.

It was an afternoon I had to lease one of the units on the 16th Floor.

Inspection of every inch so as to know how to present the property.

I found it by coincidence as was a door in the middle of nowhere locked and pulling me towards it.

It was me and the property manager

I'm trying to open door by all break and enter options available.

First the security key, didn't open, the AB key, didn't open, my special key that opens most doors, didn't open, the credit card maneuver, almost had it.. (bodgy door and lock as it was..), grabbed the screw driver from my handy kit.. 'Pop' got it open.

Aaaaahhhhh Freeedom on the 17th floor, 360' of bliss uninterrupted 'Elizabeth Bay' views. Wild but gentle water views, fresh green grass, in a Titan Developed Town.

Recharged our selves, and closed the thing to come back another day."

The End

THE VIEW FROM GEORGE ST BALCONY

"Some may 'know' some may 'not', however there is a 'penthouse property' in Sydney; when you stand on the balcony, facing True North, in line with George St, it's nothing short of the ancient film and movie the parade through the city.

Further looking out and 'zoning in' jumping from 'Century' to 'Century', seeing the 'picture before my eye's' 'and' parade and festival of 'King George', in his (Blood Red Army General Decorated with Yellow Patterns and Royal Metal Buttons suit) riding through, (west bound) on his Horse and Carriage on George Street; as people on either side cheering and waving."

The End

SWIMMING POOL

"[Summer, 'Saturday' morning, open house inspection]

All types of friends, in 'shorts' and 'bikini's' and some 'topless' splashing about and playing 'Netball' in the pool.

The End

SUN-BAKING

'Early to inspection so decided to sun bake on the rooftop infront of crystals clear pool'.

The End

SWIMMING POOL

"LOL, This one still makes me laugh.

The one that stands out from the crowed is the swimming pool that D_______ K_______ was chilling in the one in famous TV serious U_________

It was pretty high up on an open outdoor area of the Building. Cool Pool.

It was easy to hack into, (had the keys to the building and everything). Every night before bed, I'd think how cool we'd be if we got together at 'night' and just had a mad get together at the pool).

Only took a chick or two to inspect once or twice, during the day and last inspection 6:30 - 7pm. Never got the heat enough to do a 'Nudey Run' and 'jump in' although I've played a 100 minimum house party's in my mind.

Had my own 4 Star Pool at home ???

The End

GIRLFRIEND AT WORK

"That was a 'good day'; 'not 'really' a funny day but a 'memorable one'.

It was after 'months' and 'months' of being single and working. (Life was ok though :-D)

It was an 'interesting' experience, for once in my life, I was getting urges I never knew I had.

More to the point I was lonely and in need of love.

That ((week)) I met the most [beautiful and gorges 'glimmer'] ok 'glamour', as the word suggests; 'glamorous' (but sounds like someone's saying or derives from glimmers before one's eye's, doesn't it), [Glamour]. To me it always has.. Anyways , girl I have ever laid eyes on.

It was true; I had not known true beauty till that night.

Well that week that same girl, ended up being my girlfriend and further more picked me up from work (how cute); wearing 'nothing' ok, not 'nothing', but 'beauty' of a white top and flower blossoming type dress, knee length 'Lambda Dress'.

I did the 'wait 5 min I'm busy', 'surfed the net', picked her up and walked off in the sunset for the afternoon."

The End

THE GARGOYLES AND REAPERS

"This time was not as vivid, very faint, (after bad day), was walking down 'K_____ St, with head hung low, I look up to see the sky, 'Gargoyles' alive although stone, (go figure, tickle me pink) guarding the old Newtown Post Office Building.
Crouching on the clock tower, 'Growling' and 'Smiling'. Within that zone, 'demon reaper' just flying across the sky, first one 'big one', then other smaller one's criss crossing in the sky, 'one laughing at me with his 'pearly white' skeleton teeth'."

The End

OVERSEAS

"(Ha, 'this one', hats off to my older brother this guy pulls angles and equations as though 4 unit maths, (wile in 'university' 'hardly working' on an International 'overseas' 'exchange student' program, he had a unit in the 'city').

At same time I organized myself, however got 'accommodation paid' invite to go Europe.

'Minutes' away to my 'other citizenship' to see my family I hadn't seen in 11 YEARS.

The thought of (reuniting with family was a dream from the time we got separated).

Freed from 'desire' and 'commitment' in a 'new world' a 'fresh garden of eve', to do with 'my' time, 'what I want' 'as I want'.

For 4 weeks for the first time on my own in 25 Years (not including, school holidays and family holidays).

If you haven't realized by now, I felt as though I have hit the jack pot and won in life.

Landing on 'safe' and lovely/'land' was my first priority; after 18 something hours of flying at 40,000 feet altitude, 1000km's/8,500 knots an hour (cruising speed).

Once arrived, lost: from not knowing left from right to not knowing 'East from South' but it was cool there were signs.

From hot lovely weather to bellow 0' freezing snowing conditions. 'Completely 'different' 'stage and level' in my 'ultimate' 'personal' 'game', take over the 'world'; just like J____ P____ and the fellows loL

Gob smacked, the picture perfect don of fresh snow, falling on a world class city, was worth every penny, and reaching natural, magic dust, euphoric state.

Explored for days, what it is to explore ?"

The End

"The 'flip tern' up side 'down', (4 weeks holiday but with intentions to stay for 6 to 12 months, travel around Europe 'all above board').

Although while there, had 'earge's and desires' to forget about that 'plan' (travelling Europe and every single country in it) 'like the friend who sparked the idea and inspired me'. (The record states this traveler, D_____ had a [Local Beer] at every 'single country' in Europe; did it all making ends meat along the way. Took him a full year. True Story, he had the spark as though true story, but I've been galabul before.

Then he tried to convince me every country in the world.. 256 or something, I said, 'that's it', 'thanks', but I got work to do', however, honest, fit, reliable 30 year old.

Anyways, I think (do I take on this big challenge and call hun and 'let her in' and finally tell her I've done the 'runner' to 'Europe' for a year or forget that dream/plan and settle down and get 'married' to hun).

(That was it for me, I didn't want to play the player game after 25; that's why I did all the shit I did to get it out of my system, to be a good husband and father and not to have to do it in a committed relationship. Like the story's following this chapter. How little I knew myself).

'Hun calls from 'Aussy', how's things, this that, "BB I love you, come back, come back to me, I love you" over the 7 sea's.

I'm back in Syd. I explain to hun how much I missed her too and how much I love her. How I'm back and scraping the leap year in Europe I want to be with you forever no matter what, lets 'just do it' ? NIKE STYLE. Get married. 'Standing'.

'Few days later T____: "there's something I have to tell you" that I didn't mention'; (M___ (something while I was on my Dream Catching Miracle Managed, 'Holiday', that would never happen again and that would have changed my mind on all levels for continuing my life in Europe... ((With new Europe chicks to chase...))

"""""should let you know, I don't '"love'" you anymore"""""".

Shattered, she couldn't tell me this before I left for the holiday????, while asking her repeatedly "now is the time you tell me, are we in it forever or not??", now is the time you tell me, are we in it or not...? (As I have intentions to stay for 6 to 12 months)

'Threatening to burn my tickets and vowing to kill me if I go.. Acting like she can't breath without me.

"Or over the phone at least"

"I'm going on my 'bucks night' I'll be back in 4 weeks!! or (staying there for 6 to 12 months) now is the time you tell me 'honestly', am I the person you can't live without???, (as the saying goes) ""one doesn't move in/ marries someone one can 'live' with! However one Move's in/ Marries someone one can't live without'". If we talking Marriage

"Come back my love this that..." from across the sea's, my foot.

I'm stuck no job as tolled boss MR GREAT GRAND PA to fill my role 'no matter what' as was leaning to do the runner, but changed my mind on technicality, also if coming back, (was qualified and licensed now for targeting bigger company's and starting, 'Sales')

On 'mortgage repayments' and 'mortgaged up to my teeth' , would have leased it in a week, if on holidays, income cool, 'continue onwards' but I'm back now and need a place to live..

All dilemma's over what 'passwords and locks' I've given this cumbo X________

'All 'dilemmas' over how could be so 'stupid' as to 'believe' that chick 'loved me' how could I fall for the dumbest of moves; I haven't been in love since 'primary school' and that kept me in check.

I knew I go GAGA I mean 'shmako wako' 'don't know what day it is' (when in love); so I kept myself in check through exercises and exercise.

But we/both let our guards down a little we did, anyways all the trust I had ever learnt to trust in people went out the window that day; it was back to (primary rules), 'no trust and no in love with 'girls' people or 'women'.

Thank god my brother's and friend's hadn't forsaken me although we sure had to split hairs with who's who's... This that. Even our circle of friends got affected and cracked.

"Only, further to that, pulled a muscle during my 'gym training'.

(Fucking half an invalid now)

'No Chick', 'No Job', 'Torn Muscle', 'Up to my teeth in debt', 'Mentally Screwed' and 'no Good Parents/Experience in this area to support me'.

(Fucking made due with what I could, scraping by from fucked up job to more fucked up job.)

Dying for air like fish out of water just deeper and deeper down the black hole I kept going.

Uncle Sam

"Long Time ago, 18/03/06 arrived from Kuler Lumpur, interchange section, from Amsterdam, to Sydney.

I was in my Bedroom in E__________, centered in a 'North/West' pillow 'Head' position, always! OR 'North/East' was it LOL; to be in a position for best possible 'dreams' position, (based on Fairytales),
and to get the morning sunlight based on fact and 'Solar System'.

'This day the sun did not rise in the morning or afternoon, (only realizing at 19:30 on a Saturday), after having my soul lifted so 'high up' to the 'ceiling', knowing: (once passed the ceiling, there's no way back to body as soul will not be able to pass back down the concrete, only goes up; pulled by a 'Black Mist', drawing me closer and closer to his face, releasing me at the 'brink' of the 'last second' of what my 'spirit ghost' new was 'last seconds' of 'life', only for the fact, (not wanting to, but forced to) 'negotiate a deal'
at that moment, that split second; only that moment, a 'calm' and 'mercy' look, came over a face at back of 'Black Mist' and let me go, plunging down back in my soul, waking up gasping and gasping for air.

(Instead of shaking in my boots, I put my boots back on and off to a party I went).

"I recovered somewhat but wasn't fit to manage or sell Real Estate, believe it or not, one has to be in pretty fit and clear state of mind, sharp and organized". I had an injury."

The End

SO I ENROLLED IN UNI FURTHER MY EDUCATION AND KNOWLEDGE
WILE RECOVERING
(VALUATION)

"I had 'some vision' 'some perspective' 'some idea' as to 'recover my soul' and plan to bounce
back."

So, I managed.

'Sure I went to the park and 'screamed my lungs out'.I needed someone to reply!!! however no
one did;

I felt a change in the wind though.

I wasn't use to keeping a diary like now. Or (Talking to myself at times avoid putting pen to
paper)."

The End

STARTED UNI

"This was a 'mad time', a whole new chapter and back at school after '6 years' out of school.

At start it was a 'breeze' and 'fun times' compared to 'work' but hard subjects and lots to learn, TERABYTES AND TERABYTES of information.

'Fucking old dog getting taught new tricks.. It was an eye opener'.

Classic meeting and forming, some nice (life long friends).

Some parts are like in the 'movies' the set up, huge big lecture rooms, cozy chairs and Individual tables for each selective and sharp student, front and centre the lecturer's desk and projector.

([Overpriced] education was my first thought's)

'Shortly' in the term there were more In-depth topics and chapters.

(I was starting to be happy I continued on).

'Learning 'all sorts' of 'new tricks' and 'sources' of information.

But the old, 'code of manners' was too much to 'bear'.

As was in my late 20's couldn't say "how high" at the 'mark' of 'jump by the Lecturer's' and was too immature to relate to them so did what I could; studied hard and hoped for the best.

The 'exam's came', got 'top marks' in my (Residential Valuation) "Subject"/ Sorry they said jump again/ "module"; and flunked everything else.

I said (that's that for me, I'm not paying another $40,000 to do the same shit three times).

(Place that money on what I know, become a self made millionaire before the times up for me having to pay off these debts).

So I professionally and with no prejudice handed in my notice."

The End

BEST DAY

"Now came the 'time' back on my 'feet', 'sharp as ever', a 'scar on my soul', but with further TERABITES of experience, I was ready.

Registered my business and started trading without 'tools' and 'resources'. Just me, myself and I.

With 'sixth sense' of knowing not sure when or where but knowing, could sense it since I was '17' then again at time of "'Tafe Fire Alarm'" and again at time of dilemma with 'X'.

Saying it out loud even, as never have but did in the 'park that night' screaming and wishing to find that person I've been sensing all these years. 'Why me', 'Why me' why you doing this to me?' 'let me find my own client' , [A Real Life Geni-ous].

'A Geniu I've been sensing for some time, "I know his out-there, I can see him, I'm so close, I'm so close"

Registering my own business as Job Vacancy Role's where filled, searching for days and for months, walking to appointments, driving in the harshest of winds u have ever experienced, hunger and thirst like never before.

Only to find not that but something just as good.

A Molti-Billion Dollar Developer with more vacant units then I could keep count on with a computer.

I could finally hold my head up high, walk with 'Giants"; but never, ever, in any of my wildest fantasies and daydreams, would I or could I, imagine or hear of a Man, (Godfather type) that can accomplish so so much, in one life.

He is 'one' in a Trillion and it really felt as though working for a world famous STAR.

Visions of mingling and socializing with singers, actors, movie stars, people of political positions, local and international, the world was at reach once again.

[[[[And so it was]]]

I was given a 2nd chance.

Someone heard me at the park that night."

Now days all I do is sit behind the comfy chair and wait for the roger roger call.

"Roger Roger two blonds headed your way"

To be continued .... The End .

FOOTY AFTER PARTY SINGLE

"((2005 give or take a year, the night the South Sydney Rabbitohs beat the St George Dragons in the charity shield game))".

"Group of friends got together and celebrated the night out. Some cheering as the team won some upset as their team lost. All in all it was a mad game and we were at the stadium to watch it too.

Later in the night, things got 'frisky', we had started drinking up and getting drunk at a J______ house.

There was a 'pool, few of us got together and in the hot night, 'diving and jumping around we went'.

Cooling down and checking out the Cold water Spa, we got to chatting and catching up a little more.

A chick, X______ for this story, eyeing me out and me back at her, all day and night.

Flirting from time to time.

Back at the apartment.

Out of nowhere D____ comes out, towel over his shoulder, full montey, butt naked, love muscle showing, 'who's up for a swim in the pool or orgy or something'

I bust him, [just out of the room I'm trying to start my own show] as I hear him, fo fum, fo fum, 'Giant' going eat something something; R______, J______, P______ others______ all in stitches laughing out loud at the prank, and back to my I went to start up the fun.

Playing and flirting with X_____ for this story, who's been eyeing me out all night. Soaking and shorts dripping wet with water from the 'pool', 'no towel', 'wet' and 'in front of her'; jump wet in the bed, mate upset later on! (me too upset at myself for that), however had to take some risk not to break the 'mood and momentum' had to be there... you don't go "((let me dry up change ask my mate for dry clothes keep that look and thought I'll be back in 30 to 45 min...))"

I jumped on the bed and 'took her on', 'wet and slippery' and we fucked till I dried up.

Wooshka, in came D____, R_____, and J_____ busting us. Me thinking there doing the same in the other room.. 'Only to see them 3 or 4 staring at me, as I jumped up and under covers I went, shied up in shock, 'sprung', saying we'll be out in a minute.

They close the door and 'on' I kept going. All the while wanting to come out and share (as was that type of party) but the pull of the sex was so intense; the one on one was so entrapping with one and other it was too wearied to wreck the moment, as if we went from fucking to making love to fucking again."

The End.

"(OMG), she was a 'Hotty', a night out on my own, as tired of friends meeting up then wanting to go somewhere else or one can't get in and so on, one night on my own.

In the middle of the club we were drunk and smashed off our rocks; just after the good old days where 10 schooners a night was a minimum.

'Dancing' and moving the 'suddle' 'two steps' as she was dancing on the stage; 'white mini skirt' and 'yellow tank sports bra top' "(what do they call em)" 'tank sports top'; Anyways, nice toned female she was, mix of 'Sheila'/Zena, mellow look but the attitude was there..

She's dancing without a 'care' in the world, I'm mesmerized and 'turned on' and 'actually thankful for the moment' as was punching above my weight.

Doing 'twirls', dancing to energy music, and in tune with music fit thing.

Light brown/ dark hazel hair colour with sunshine blonde wavy streak's in hair, with, pony tail, and then let loose and natural dancing as she was.

I'm bedazzled, 'happy to just catch a glimpse of her 'box' in 'white mash with bits of sea through lingerie' as was dancing right underneath the stage.

I call her down to dance she says

"I'm having fun",

I go (ill try my luck and go on stage), 'dance for a little' (but not doing my older days dance on stage hog the floor moves, just aham aham two step, stage shy that night for some reason).

Few eyes from the club on me, nice sometimes but wasn't in that mood.

'Anyways' I jump back down and call her down instead.

Alibaba Smile, "Just come down for a while, less spot light' wink.

She jumps down and starts dancing with me, we got a bit closer and rubbed a few times.

Normally and in all cases, I keep the dancing going and fun rolling as long as I can, however I knew when to calm down and chill for a while; just played the silent shy type sipping my drink at a table watching her.

Few guys made moves, man I was dirty, few stink eye's flew, and maybe a suddle threat of a slap, as was at par or even bigger than most that night, as older that was all; however (can't stop people trying on a beauty), she turned them down, I'm sure she saw the relief on my face.

I was in heaven, the night was good.
X_____ for this story, kept turning down guys as I was sipping on my drinks and drinking with her from time to time; the night only got older, the club was closing before we knew it. As the club was shutting we walk out together although X___ At a dilemma with me, she knew what I wanted, I'm pretty straight about the fact, although (she was out to get laid that night too), she was eyeing out someone else as well, with more money and shiny belt, as though they know each other from another night.

I snapped her out of it with a good 'wake up to yourself' and offered to 'walk her home'; as she lived 'few doors down' from the club learning from the conversations.

Off we go, beautiful charmed house too, In through the front door, (I'm in, I'm home) I said to myself, 'up the stairs to her bedroom', 'as she's pulling me by the hand', in the dark, with mobiles as light.
As she's walking up the stairs, I say 'lets just do it hear', 'ok' I take her G sting off, lift her skirt up, I spread those legs, gliding inside of her, as though perfect hip to hip ratio."

The End

""(At the local park bench with D____, M_____ S____ and B_____ as his walking his K9.)""

""This 'Guy', medium height, some call 'Large', some 'Short', 'crew cut' at the front with light 'maine hair' at the back, black 'maine', suddle glow of silver and gold, nice features, distinctive and strong eye brows, sharp eye's, sharp nose, soft and defined cherry red lips, a million dollar smile and pearly natural white teeth with 2 defined fangs; tight but tender muscle tone and skin.

Body 'Swimmer' athletic, with broad shoulders, medium to athletic arms as guns V style torso, 32 inch waist hips, and legs like 'Adonis'.

His best feature was his 'oversized', popping out the centre of his body, well and perfectly developed and defined muscle.
'Chubby' or 'Hard', always pumping and throbbing with raw hot blood and can measure ones heart beat, as though a life of its own.

This guy on this one Saturday night, decided to go out to town in Sydney, with the same goals and ideas, any one guy would have reading or writing such a story; to get laid or get paid not necessarily always in that order.

The night was young and one was bursting with beautiful clean energy, sourced from the clear black night, moon light and stars in the sky, a slow and steady night, when in tune with the rotation of the earth.. you may have experience such a night, everything is in tune.

'Walking' and 'Talking' warming up our body's, getting that pump you get from warming up, (our tricks and trades), trying to reach irresistibility and (often succeeding) but hard to perform always body mind and spirit need to be in tune as they were on this night.

We pick a club, the best and brightest only, [although an old ancient venue], heard story's of the young [Navy officers partying from the hey days], but still kicking and will kick on for years to come, story for another book.

With meet and greet passed security, not my cozens, lucky ducky and paki, so the quick sly of the hand $20.00 hand shake.

D_____ and I, find a good position, to blend in with the crowed or stand out depending on our mood; at the bar as we first order drinks, as a habit, but not always in that order.

The place was dark with few dim lights, and a dance floor.

Expensive Venue to say the least but lots of commoners attend.

Started putting out and tuning up the vibe, as J_____ use to say..

With subtle look's and wink hear, flash there, sign over there, 'The guy' managed to grab a girl by the arm, force her to the wall and get with her 'French Kiss Style'; loving it back as she was.. we kissed and kissed for hours.
Hot voluptuous lips, fresh breath, mint crisp, tongues deep in each other's mouth, sloppy at times with teasing each other on who will kiss again, leading to subtle touches' caressing her tight young body, gently going up and down her thighs, teasing and teasing her inner thighs, rubbing my hard muscle against her pumped and throbbing jelly pussy, praying to myself she doesn't back out.

I get interrupted by mate off we go to another club.. 'Exchanged numbers' and we said we'le keep in touch.

At other bar now, also a swave and elegant a renovated job bar with all the bells and whistles but lot quiter; we have another drink.

Before setting out the vibe we get approached, ok, 'girls of ours' came to say hi.

Off the start, wasn't playing games that night was in tune with rotation of the earth, I say, as a joke, let me see your 'tits', so she flashed me; my favoret line, "munch munch, pussy for lunch loL", NAAA and to close who ever loved that not loved at first sight, (Romeo); with that finished my drink and asked her to come for a walk with me outside for fresh air and cig."

Leaving D_____ with his chick as they were pretty into each other, as though they've done that dance before and a bit of peace and quiet.
I'm outside, I start talking and aurising her with sweet nothing's, 'joke hear, joke there', (focusing on erotic and arising topics and planting images in her mind, sassing out my boundaries).

With full 'sweet surrender' J______ lets me take her to the hidden away stair way of somebody's house loL.. 'People don't try this at home'. 'I gently ask her to go all the way with me' , she lifts up her skirt, takes her G string under her dress and puts it on the floor. She carkes one leg up and face on standing we go at it on each other. Soft warm and cozy, wet and dripping at the spontaneous of moments, we went on for half an hour moaning and screaming.
I'm pumping all the way with my balls half in, wam the owner of the house comes outside with flash torch light what you's doing there.

'Oh, shit'

Quickly pull out and back on the street we continued happy as Larry and rejuvenated and re energized feeling even better than before; ready to take more off the night.

We tried to reconnect with friends, friends in bar weren't there; I called 'no answer', 'busy doing their thing'.
I say to X______ for this story, wait hear for them, I guess; I gotta go to my car and top up the meter or would you like to come with me ? With all intentions to top up my parking meter off I went as she chose to stay at bar.

(No fine), 'thank god', (top up the meter), done.

(Now relax unwind in my car for a little, reflecting on what a mad time it was).

Still horny and throbbing as didn't finish, I want to find relief, I did the old (chat up the first chick that comes while standing next to my car).

One group went passed, (waited for the second).

The second group was 'two females' and a guy.

Whistle, 'you hold on a minute',(mature women in her late 30's), 'I need to ask you something'.

She say's "its fine go on ill catch up", to her friends, off they went.
Taking a 'risk' although she was looking at me as she wants to eat me alive.

[I place my full hand on her mad pumped pussy in reply].

"Lets hang in the car for a while, wile we get to know each other"

'Open the car door in we go'.

Talking and getting to 'know' each other; we got to talking to what sort of 'dicks' she likes.

'Right into it', 'why don't you show me yours'; [still hard and pumping I pull out a throbbing cock and flash her in the car].

Aroused and excited as it was her 'type'; she sais "can I touch it", 'sure I said', "you know I'd love a head job'. Wam off to work she went.

Tying up and saying our fair wells. Sun was starting to come out.

Still horny I call up the 'first girl' the one was kissing at the club; to see how her night is and (see if she wanted to hook up).

As I'm 'talking' with her, she says I just got off the bus in R________ I am headed home.

I said "stop right there", "wait for me", " I can be there in '20 min' to have coffee and breakfast; and a kiss, what you think ?"

I'm driving in no traffic, early morning sun beautiful and bright, (was for a mad day to begin).

I call again and confirm location, she's on main road, I see her and pick her up.

We pulled up at the lookout, tired from the night, coffee time "how was your night", how was your night" off to business we get. In the car, bumping and grinding.

I dropped her off home and 'then' home; to get some sleep and try and do it all again like Vince and Nick next week.""

The End

MIRROR

A 'wile' back not so anymore but maybe earlier tonight, I use to look in the mirror dead straight at myself, serious as hell, and really, 'say out loud':

" Mirror Mirror on the wall who is the fairest of them all"

I'd always get, your brother is, or the other Stars in the area is, 'one time no word of a joke', the time I could feel a thousand hearts beating and cheering me on the mirror said you are you coincided son of a gun.

Only to reach a level of static to see an electric spark ignite from my index finger.

"(My lord, I've done it)"   "(Na that wasn't big enough) But convinced myself (I come from that line).

Let's do it again, come on, come on, the vision and spark was gone.

The End

ISBN 978-0-9953982-0-7
9 780995 398207